AELINA ISAACS

Prince of Sylvan

Prequel to The Eternal Machine

First published by Aelina Isaacs 2021

Copyright © 2021 by Aelina Isaacs

This novel is entirely a work of fiction. The names, characters and incidents portrayed in it are the work of the author's imagination. Any resemblance to actual persons, living or dead, events or localities is entirely coincidental.

Aelina Isaacs asserts the moral right to be identified as the author of this work.

First edition

ISBN: 978-1-7378285-6-3

This book was professionally typeset on Reedsy.
Find out more at reedsy.com

To all those who save themselves from the depths of the murky ocean called life.

Contents

Preface

Please read before starting your adventure with Prince of Sylvan.

This is an **adult** fantasy fiction novel with queer romance which includes mature themes such as violence and sex, which are described in graphic detail. **Mature themes** include descriptions of physical and verbal abuse, references to past sexual assault.

I highly recommend reading The Eternal Machine, the first novel in the series, before reading this book if you don't want certain mysteries to be spoiled. However, this can be read on it's own as well.

If you enjoy reading in a chronological fashion, the correct order is in the back of this book.

Iverbourne

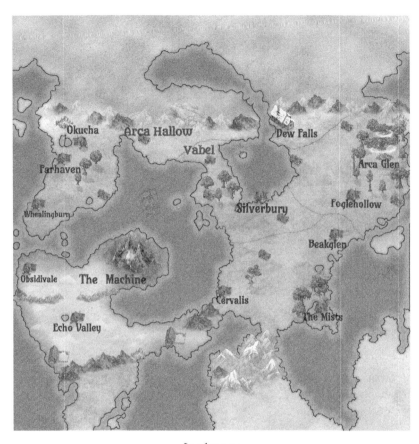

Iverbourne

Old Language

Old Language

The Old Language is based on the Hebrew language, some words are adjusted to fit the story.

Ai - an agreement

nafshyi - psychic soliders

zemer - a great musician

benzonna - son of a whore

nagid - great leader

te'omin - the twin princes

ahuvi - my love

lavaya - funeral rites

l'shanah tovah tikatevu - May it be written in the stars you have a good year.

l'aryik - the banishing

tannin - dragon

Hakol missetader kemo shetsarikhe - Everything has a way of working out.

I

Silverbury

You're going soft.

⁂

Silverbury, Sylvan Court
16,074 A.C

"Prince, there's blood on your lapel."

With a snap of my fingers, violet Aether sparks from my eyes and reflects in the female's before me. Steaming water targets the crimson splash and lifts it from my otherwise spotless suit. A deep sigh leaves me and the petite Fae curtsies before leaving, layers of gossamer and tulle crumpling around her as she does.

"Tonight." Charis whispers on her way past, long tresses of strawberry blonde sweeping behind her. The only acknowledgment I give the rebellious noble is the perking of my charcoal tufted ears. I straighten on the dais, my eyes trained on the sea of nobility filling the crystalline ballroom below.

The High Lord lounges on one of his many sizable thrones, this one studded with diamonds and sapphires. Surprisingly, Typhan has a semblance of a shirt on tonight, and the layers of necklaces adorned with beads and bones bounce with each boisterous laugh. Several young Human women are draped across him, his typical type. Thin

3

with fair skin and hair, my Mother's contrast.

Mother isn't at his side, and Orion isn't here either. My heart thunders as I realize where he must be. I wait in place to the far right of the High Lord, hands clasped tight behind my back while the latest wave of Fae flatters their Court. My charming mask of Prince is on, though I hope there isn't anymore blood lingering on me from the torture session this afternoon. Typhan glances sideways at me several times, his exuberantly false smile revealing glimpses of fury.

Once the last round of nobility offers their thanks to the High Court, I stride to Typhan's side with my hands still tight behind my back. A long haired woman is seated in his lap and nibbles on the bare point of his pointed ear. The High Lord laughs, his massive hands traveling up her slender bare thigh. I clear my throat and avoid the drugged eyes of the slave hungering for her captor.

"Father, shouldn't Orion be here?" I muse. I don't dare ask if Mother should be, I know the answer to that. Typhan waves me off dismissively and strokes his beard, his array of rings and necklaces reflecting the brilliant chandlers of faelights above. The human's eyes glaze further and she stares blankly at me. I swallow fear in anticipation of the daily murderous nudge coming from my Father.

"You and I both know your brother isn't High Court material, why bother when he won't be around much longer, eh?" My jaw tightens and I stiffen under his hard pale gaze, neck throbbing with fury and chained power. The white vine tattoos glowing along my bare arms and neck give away my intention, and Typhan smirks. He slides the woman off his lap and gingerly rises from his throne, then squeezes my shoulder tight.

"Alvis, why do you keep fighting your destiny? You know who the Aether is going to choose for my next heir," He leans closer and whispers into my ear, "So why not just get it over with? Think of what you can do with his power, and your own is already so great ..."

Typhan caresses my cheek tenderly and I shake under my father's touch, just the thought of being separated from my twin has my stomach twisting. Burning flesh fills the air around us, the blood bond between us ever present in my simmering tattoos. His matching set is glowing as well, but he delights in my self torment.

"Even thinking about killing me will set you ablaze, as it should."

"One day you'll understand, and one day you won't be able to say no, which may be coming sooner than you think. And I do wonder, where *is* your Mother gallivanting off to tonight?" He murmurs, straightening the collar of my shirt.

"No doubt at the Lake, you know how she despises these things." I say with a snarl, glancing at his throne. The humans are now practically crawling across the dais, clinging to every part of my father they can. Typhan shoves his tongue down the throat of the woman who had been in his lap and grasps her breast, his other hand diving into her hair. I cannot leave without him saying so, nor look away.

I glare at the sight and bury my moral compass, a cry emits from the small thing when he rips at her breast and tears what little clothing she had, fingers digging into thin skin. Humans are fragile to begin with, and they never last long with Father. Typhan's lips drown out her pain as flesh separates from her chest, but I can't take it anymore. I draw the long sword from my back and grip the handle like I would a lover, gentle but commanding.

Blood pours through the hall, his fingers have transformed into claws and her torso is ripped open. Despite the fatal wound she is now laughing under his attention, oblivious to her plight, and my father to his. I shove my Father's shoulder backwards and thrust my blade into his poisonous heart, sending him to the ground. I straddle his abdomen and twist with both hands, watching the light fade from his eyes with satisfaction rolling through my soul.

Body wrenching pain jolts me to reality.

A Prince of a land known for its prejudice and blood lust, brought to his knees before his High Lord, bested by his own hatred. Typhan pulls away from his slave, her clothes ripped but skin intact, and contemplates me with a smirk. I can never kill him in this reality, not without breaking the bond, and he knows I never will. My fantasy has transformed the once white tattoos into spiraling tendrils of burns, deep and searing.

"As much fun as this is, be off with you, find your Mother before I do."

* * *

Crystalline halls transform into stone walls, windows and the outside world disappearing. Darkness thickens as faelights dwindle, and soon there is nothing but the sound of my own footsteps. A simple wooden door waits for me in the nothingness burrowed under the castle above, and my hand pauses on the handle. I glance behind me at another door embedded in the side stone wall, the dungeons I spent my morning in, and most days.

Orion's inner shields are down, he hasn't sensed me yet and I can feel everything pouring from his spirit without even being in the same room. His emotions crash through our bond, sorrow and frustration twisted with despair. I strengthen my wall between us, something we never needed as children. To feel all your own pain, and that of your other half, is a burden I cannot physically carry all of the time.

And we both have too many secrets from each other, now.

With a deep exhale I turn the handle and enter the dim Aether Lab. Innocuous at first, industrial work tables and apothecary supplies fill the landing area. Jars and terrariums fill the lofty space, covering stone walls and several long iron and wooden tables. Bright flowers and exotic plants beg you to sate your curiosity and take a closer look, though I know better.

Despite the Air Fae servants creating ventilation to the outside world at the expense of their own health, the atmosphere is thick with tincture chemicals, parchment and death. I pause in the center of the room upon seeing Orion on the other end of the expansive lab. Charcoal hands grip either side of the archway holding the closed Doorway of Death, as I call it, his shaking body refusing to leave what's inside. Four young slaves are present, a pale and sickly body occupying each corner of the room.

The day Orion learned Air Fae can purify poisonous air by simply exchanging it through their own magic infused lungs was made much worse by the fact I tried to hide one important piece of information. The scars along my back tingle with shame every time I lock eyes with one of them.

Children who have just gone through the Spark purify the air at twice the rate adults do and somehow manage to survive the fatal effects twice as long, though they suffer all the same.

"You are dismissed." I order, removing the glove from my left hand before I extend it into the air thick with death before me. One by one the skeletal children with skin reminiscent of bodies floating in bog water much too long, flee from their posts. The eldest takes my hand first and I immediately have to stifle a cough as Aether leaves my skin and absorbs into her own, but I keep my eyes on Orion still frozen at the doorway.

I've learned over time I can only give just enough Aether to bring the color back to their faces and restore some of the air in their broken bodies. In the past, I've over done it and nearly exposed myself, and more importantly, them. As the last child takes my fingers blackened by their poison, I finally return my attention to the four of them. The eldest, a purple haired Fae with silver eyes, opens her cracked lips, only to be interrupted by a fatal glare from me.

"I *said*, you are dismissed, don't make me ask twice." I snap, ears folded down against my neck. Her lips twinge upwards but she hurriedly rushes the other servants out, and the door softly shuts behind them. I have a feeling they're siblings, but I'm better off not knowing. I slide the leather glove over a now entirely blackened hand, then rake back my coils before crossing the room to my paralyzed brother.

I rest a hand on his slender shoulder trapped in a bloody cream tunic, and a shock of sadness surges through me. Orion shoves me away and steps back, shakily combing crimson hands through his loose inky locks. Though he's my twin, we couldn't be more different. We're both quite tall fellows with matching near charcoal skin and textured inky hair like Mother's, but the white vine tattoos lining both of us match Father.

"You'll be sick again tonight." He chides.

"I'm already sick in the head, nothing new." I attempt to play, but he glares at me. It's not that he doesn't care for the Air Fae, he just doesn't see the point. "I'm sorry I couldn't be here, I think he's trying to keep me away from you lately."

"It's nothing." Orion says, composing himself whilst throwing his hair up into its usual low knot. I run a gloved hand through my own curls once more, the length on my crown contrasting the cropped sides. My subtle show of rebellion against Typhan.

"You're allowed to feel something when they don't make it." I whisper, extending a hand between us. Orion laughs, his violet eyes flaring as he bellows. I've never been afraid of my scrawny brother, but the instability in his eyes these past few months has me worrying. We are both nearing our breaking points.

"We are monsters, no matter how much it *hurts*, no matter how many Fae you try to save, no matter how much I feel. You cannot simply wash away evil with good intentions."

I open my lips, but have no idea what to say He's not wrong, even sharing my Aether with those kids is just prolonging an inevitable end to their miserable life here.

Is there a right or wrong when you're living in hell?

"I love you, O." I whisper over the bond to him. I offer my hand again, he takes it and I yank him into my chest. His filthy leather apron taints my fine suit adorned with medals and gaudiness. I allow hot tears to fall for a moment whilst he's not looking, both of us embracing so tight around the other we shake. He smells awful, his work leathers are saturated in blood and chemicals. My little brother, by three minutes as he likes to remind me, a mad scientist.

And I, his dutiful lackey.

"You and me, that's how we live." Orion whispers the motto we crafted when we were kids, and have promised the other everyday since. I swallow my fear and nod, holding him tighter. Orion steps back at once as if shocked and crosses his arms, raising an angled brow. What he lacks in musculature he makes up for with stubbornness, I'll give him that.

"You're sad, why are *all* your walls up?"

"It's nothing, I'm just worried about Mother, have you seen her?" I admit half the truth, but Orion's well trained mask of indifference falls over his sharp face as footsteps approach behind me.

"Well? Let me guess, you need another one." Apollo drawls, thrusting a hand onto each of our shoulders with the same dangerous comfort Typhan impresses. He is dressed in silks, oceanic blues and silvers complementing his pale and sharp features. Exquisite jewelry adorns his ear points, neck and arms.

He wants to be Father so much it makes me sick.

"Splicing Aether is incredibly difficult, and changing nature's course has consequences, something you know nothing about." Orion states matter of factually, lilac flashing in his hard eyes. Apollo's pale hands squeeze tight and I shrug him off, as does Orion. Apollo laughs, his fair features remind me of his mother that Typhan so easily used and discarded for another son.

Just in case I fail.

"Spare me the bullshit, the group you made last year were performing at stellar levels. Wouldn't you say, Al? After all, you're the one who trained them." Apollo jabs, and I flinch under the reminder. The original *Nafshyi* truly were grand science experiments, the only Air Fae who survived the Water Aether injections and my months long process of breaking them. Molded into dutiful psychic forces of nature that can break your mind in an instant.

The first raid I did with them to collect stray Fae in the rural lands ended horribly, what should've been a covert abduction ended as an entire village massacred. The delight and amusement their self proclaimed leader held for bloodshed was not something I foresaw, nor their ability to fight the bonds keeping them in line. Orion didn't hold back when creating those super soldiers, there was too much on the line, and we hadn't been beaten down by our conscience, yet.

Now, his hesitance is going to get him killed, or more likely, both of us *and* Mother.

"What's your point?" I snarl.

"Point is, you're going soft, both of you. It's impeding Father's success and he's going to do something about it *very* soon, if you don't get your shit together."

Orion blinks, then speaks as if he just learned the sky was blue. "Are you, *warning* us?" Apollo shoves him against the solid wooden Doorway to Death, pinning Orion's neck with a thick arm and knocking off his glasses. I unsheathe a dagger strapped to my side and lay it to Apollo's neck, Aether bubbling in my furious heart.

"Never, I'd kill you both right now if I wasn't skinned myself for it." Apollo growls, glaring at me over his shoulder with flashing white

Aether in his hard eyes. His hard set brow is pulled tight, his broad and rugged features resembling Typhan more than we do. Orion puts his hands up in surrender, suppressing a snicker, and Apollo releases him. He straightens his elegant silk long sleeved tunic before addressing me. "I suggest you find your mother."

You're delusional.

There are several glamours I cycle through, changing with each food delivery. Illusion work is an Aether skill most common with Air Fae, though some of the more powerful Water Fae like myself can pull on a glamour.

Tonight I play the part of a typical middle aged Water Fae with light bronze skin, cropped brunette hair. My now healed bright white tattoos are not so easily glamoured, so I dress in a long sleeved charcoal tunic and thick wool cloak. Sweat dampens my collar, though the air is considered crisp by most. Cold is a welcome friend to me, something to make you feel alive.

The double moons are empty, Yule shall be the next solstice in a few weeks. I've been hoping snow will fall in Sylvan this year, though it rarely does. Tutors could never explain to me why it snows across the mainland but never here, though I suspect it has to do with a certain High Lord's magic. I silently thank the darkness for keeping me from prying civilian eyes, and the last visible sentry before I entered the slums was a few blocks back.

The Outer Rim isn't worth spying on or protecting, at least in Typhan's eyes. He takes what he wants from them when he pleases and in exchange, pays them no attention. Most of the already stretched militia is stationed at the port and along the towering walls hiding Silverbury from the world. No one enters without explicit permission from Typhan himself, and certainly no one leaves without him knowing. Even traders who come to visit suddenly find themselves trapped here, found useful by the court one way or another.

Which is why, to my surprise, there is a new ship docked at the small airport just inside the main gates, which are locked of course. I pause my hurry and observe the galleon from a distance, having to rub my eyes several times to make sure I am indeed seeing a flying *pirate* ship. And in Sylvan no less. Even in the darkness the folded golden sails shine, and the behemoth Aether engines along the bottom of the ship are remarkable.

Sylvan prides itself on having the best Aether engines, but I can tell from here those are one of a kind. I decide to investigate after I make my drop, the fully loaded hand wagon trailing behind me as I resume my journey. Cries of poverty and petty disputes rattle through the streets, and too many Fae offer to be my lover for the night. I amble through the residential slums, thankful I'm almost to my destination. A two story brick home with no roof, unremarkable in comparison to the other dwellings, most of which are in similar crumbling condition.

I scan the area before finding the wide side door, then knock. Pause, then knock three times. Pause, then tap. The door slides on it's runner just enough for me to enter and I wander into darkness, then let the wagon handle drop when the creaking door closes. "You're late!" Charis hisses, snapping her fingers to alight a singular lilac faelight.

The dirt floor storeroom I've entered is stocked full of empty crates, burlap bags and numerous cupboards, all the means to operate a store, but no food. No longer dressed in layers of nobility, Charis dons a high waisted pair of brown trousers and a plain long sleeved grey tunic, the way she usually dresses when we're breaking the law.

"I've had a night, okay?" I sigh, rubbing my unfamiliar and wide face. Charis rolls her bright blue eyes and swishes her beautiful strawberry blonde hair out of the way while she uncovers the delivery. I've asked her so many times to cut her tresses, but she always just gives me that I'd rather die look. Even after what Typhan made me to do her, she hasn't stopped fighting.

Then again, that's what he wants us all to do.

"Yes, showing up with blood on your clothes was a nice touch." She sighs with exasperation.

"It was *one* spot," I groan and hurriedly assist her with unloading the canned goods and sacks of 'no good' produce into crates, "listen, this will have to be the last time, and I won't be able to cook tomorrow. I, I brought everything I could."

As I admit defeat the words sting my soul, we've been running this kitchen together for decades, though we've had to move several times and suffer multiple punishments. Inflicted punishments on each other.

"Alvis, they won't survive!" Charis jolts in place and keeps me in her furious gaze, thin blonde brows scrunched together. She rubs her face and inhales deeply, calming her tone. "Whatever's happened, we can work around it."

"Don't you think I know that! No matter what I do, someone dies." I shout, then dim my anger to a whisper. She is before me in an instant, too gentle hands cupping my cheeks, and I sigh, her touch comforting and terrifying me at the same time. Charis is my only friend, though I wish she would've stayed out of my rebellious lure.

"He's going to make me do it Char, I just know it. Mother is disappearing more and more lately, O is losing his mind, and I just can't help but wonder if I should just go ..." I trail off and avert my glistening eyes, but she yanks my face back.

"You can't talk like that, you can't give up now after everything." Charis pleads, hands now tight on my face. I take both of her hands in mine and search her petite face for the resentment she should holds towards me, but find only concern.

"Char, you of all people know what a hold he has on me. I can't ... I can't hurt people anymore." I admit in a whisper, eyes and hands dropping. I realize she isn't breathing, and this isn't how I wanted our goodbye to go. I muster a small smile and back away, putting my hands up as I pull out my tired humor.

"I'll try my best to keep going, but only because you asked so nicely."

"Alvis, I believe in you." She says with a sad smile. I nod and push the door open, but her last words haunt me. "Thank you, for everything."

* * *

There's only one more place I can think of Mother hiding, and it's the worst. Despite my curiosity in the peculiar airship, there are more pressing matters. I truly thought her days of orchestrating rebellions were over when she nearly killed Orion and I, not to mention herself. If my tattoos weren't covered I'm sure their glow would be illuminating the finer streets I traverse through now. Dim yellow faelights line the grand cobble streets leading to the Market. Elegant mansions constructed of granite similar to the palace loom in the darkness, their lifeless windows in the night send a chill through me.

I changed glamour when I left the Outer Rim for the valley where middle and some higher class Fae live, figuring my noble but not *too* noble young Fae disguise should work quite nice. Same light bronze skin and cropped brunette hair, the wide jaw has less lines and muscles are more defined. My actual dark complexion is more common in Terra lands, not in this hellish place lining the largest body of water in Iverbourne. My breath catches in my throat as I step into the main square, the Market.

A beautiful square decorated with crystalline statutes, gardens and fountains. The expansive gathering place is encapsulated by bustling businesses, homes and taverns. The venue I'm looking for is at the opposite end, and I have no choice but to enter the fine dressed crowd blocking my way. I swallow rising panic as I realize tomorrow is the only day of the week the laborers have off, making tonight their designated cause trouble and party too much night. I cannot help but pause halfway to my destination, impatient Fae shoving past me. The raised wooden platform violating the center of the otherwise beautiful Market sends grief through me, it's simplicity contrasts the dripping wealth around it. Rows of stone pews face the platform, waiting in anticipation for tomorrow's goods to be auctioned off. The day Typhan caught Charis and I feeding 'property' scraps is one that haunts my every waking moment, and to this day bile still burns in my belly every time I see the auction block.

I sigh and continue weaving through wealthy Water Fae, my eyes averted from the pooled ruddy crimson stains surrounding the auction block. Epic quartz crystals embedded along the numerous scaling rooftops catch my eye instead, and I wonder how Typhan will replace the mining crew he slaughtered last week for not meeting their quota. Cheerful Fae and lofty unfamiliar music reaches me when I near the entrance to the Shipwreck, exotic spices entangling with fermentation and perfume.

The Shipwreck is just that, an old pirate galleon transformed into a magnificent establishment. Earth Fae servants were given a week off duties in exchange for seamlessly constructing a cottage-like building around the ship. Oceanic flags thrust upon a crows nest and along the bow of the ship are at ease, no wind to tickle their eternal rest here. A tall figure hidden by a dark blue cloak casually approaches the entrance, then darts into a side alley.

Within a split second I strengthen my glamour, blurring my figure with the shadows as I sneak up to the corner of the narrow alley, ears perking for any noise. I scan the Market in front of me, body sheltered by the Shipwreck's looming shadow, then peer around the corner. Shipping crates line the wall closest to me and I slink alongside it, pausing when I hear a melodic voice.

"This is the last time, you'll have to go on without me." Mother.

"Your work will not go unnoticed, to those who matter." The responding voice is neither male or female, a distorted version of solemn kindness.

"And my sons, they'll be safe?" Silence follows her trepidation. "Captain, you gave your word." I clench my fists and consider confronting this Captain and my ever troublesome Mother, but a good spy always listens first, and asks questions later.

"You have *my* word, though I cannot speak for my crew, several are survivors from Vabel, as you can understand this is … " gravel distortion pauses, dropping an octave, "personal."

"Trust me when I tell you, they are not their actions." Mother warns, and I can just picture her finger pointed in this Captain's face, her sharp face set tight and shoulders pulled back. I bristle with pride, but am cut short when I notice a sentry patrolling closer to the Shipwreck, and us. Shit.

I clench my hands, my poisoned fist trembling with pain. I drained so much Aether earlier, I have no choice as the sentry nearly stumbles upon me. I close my eyes and inhale, then thrust my arms towards the alley exit, straight for the Market center. With a meditative exhale, a wave of nipping and fierce horses stampede through the celebrations being held. Screams erupt and shouts echo through the flooded block, the sentry turns his back on my hidden figure and sprints to the chaos unfolding.

I smirk and release one more beast, straight for the auction platform. Neither a horse or any creature I'm familiar with, what my Aether unleashes terrifies me.

A great snakelike beast, so epic it's water-composed wingspan encompasses the width of the entire Market square. In stupid awe I step out of the alley and witness the creature land onto the auction platform, unable to comprehend what I've conjured. Tons of swirling liquid rest on strong hind legs, and front legs with massive talons smash the stone pews off to the side like toys.

"Alvis! What are you doing here!" Mother hisses from behind me, figure still in the shadows. I turn on my heel and when I see Mother's worried face, the creature collapses into rolling waves, further flooding the area.

"Go, before someone sees you!" I order in a whisper. She obeys and dissipates into thin air, using what I'm sure is the last of her Aether allotment for the day. Sirens ring through the Market and more guards fill the disastrous plaza, plucking Fae from the flood. I duck into the still bustling Shipwreck, if I travel right now I'll surely pass out. An unfamiliar tavern is waiting, there are no pearls or suits here. A grand party of working class Water Fae fills the tavern, oblivious to the destruction that awaits outside.

Usually perfectly placed tables are pushed to the side, providing more room for joyous Fae to swing each other about, dancing in a wild way I've never seen before. Cheers of *"Zemer!"* chant through the place and I take the last remaining stool at the bar, struggling to see where the odd musician is through the madness around me. The music is from a lute, but the melody is much faster than I've ever thought the instrument could manage.

I order a whiskey and slide a few extra gold coins to the dark skinned Female, her raven coils remind me of Mother. She gives me a toothy smile and slings a rag over her shoulder, then leans on the bar and raises a thick brow, knowing full well I want more than a drink.

"Pray tell, dear Onya, what are we celebrating?" I muse, attempting to speak loud enough so she can hear me but quiet enough to remain discreet. Her eyes flash a soft purple and she chuckles, familiar with my current glamour. Aether saps in my veins, my body slowly dehydrating from the inside out the longer I hold up the illusion.

"A mysterious benefactor bought out the place, insisting no 'rich assholes' were allowed." Onya raises a knowing brow, then juts her chin to where the stage is, still hidden by rows of people. As I throw back another shot, I wonder if the Shipwreck is tilting, though I doubt it. "I suspect it was that *Zemer,* won't accept tips."

"So, that means he's a mysterious benefactor, eh?" I tease, taking the next drink she slides to me. Is this number three already, or four? I can't deny the music pouring from the heart warming lute is quite uplifting, and I realize the musician hasn't stopped at all since I've entered. Onya thrusts her hands on wide flaring hips, her body dressed in brilliant gossamer blues and oranges, the deep cut neckline revealing nearly everything.

"Scrawny thing like *that* needs all the help he can get, only reason someone like that doesn't take money is because they have it."

I throw back drink number four, or five, and rise unsteadily, tapping the counter as I do.

"Guess I'll have ta find out for myself then, eh?" I scoff, slurring over my words and feet. Bless her heart, Onya sets a drink for the road on the bar and I leave her more coins than a week's worth of pay will bring, like I usually do. I squeeze through sweat drenched Fae, hands explore me at once and fingers twirl in my hair. Any other night I would meld in with the orgy and lose myself in any and every Fae because it would be *my* choice, but the music demands to be discovered.

I stumble upon arriving at the front of the crowd, surprised to find the stage is filled with dancing Fae as well. A slender male skips in a circle with a handsome brunette female, his fingers wildly plucking each note from the multitude of strings without missing a beat. How his wild harmony can be uninterrupted by his happiness filled dancing is beyond me, but joy is plain upon his, and every face in here. A mop of bouncing honey curls compliments his fair skin lighter than most Water Fae, I've never seen one with such striking sapphire eyes. The dimple filled smile lighting up the musician's face sends my heart into a flutter, but his joy falters upon connecting eyes with me. I can't tell if I'm swaying, or if the ship is finally being rocked off it's foundation. The music enters a final crescendo for the first time in over ten minutes, and clapping emits. I join in, but the musician glares at me.

Cheers erupt and fold my ears down, the noise reverberating through my dizzied mind. The bard excuses himself for a drink and I rush over to the bar, where Onya has two glasses ready. She flashes me a wink and I snatch both up, nearly falling over myself. When I turn around the mop of curls has disappeared and I frown, searching over the crowd. I settle for standing awkwardly on the side of the room, heart still beating out of my chest.

In the blink of an eye he is suddenly in front of me, sandy tunic half undone and revealing his lean chest. Blue fire alights his strong eyes and I harden, his glare burns me alive from the inside out. "Oh, hi! Erm, I mean, here," I stifle a groan and thrust a drink forward, managing to effortlessly spill it onto his simple linens, "thirsty, right?"

Get a grip Alvis, holy hell.

The bard raises a blonde brow and eyes me with suspicion, so I drink my own which leads him to throw the drink back. I grin nervously but his lips push thin, his dimples hiding. "I can see past your illusions."

Well, shit.

I open my lips but have no idea what to say, and he rolls his eyes with exasperation. I clench my fists and straighten, though alcohol may override my blood volume right now. "You're delusional, kid."

He steps closer and the magic in his eyes flares intensely, illuminating the galaxies of freckles across his cheeks. There are inches between us, and if he steps any closer he'll find out just how much a good fight thrills me. "You're delusional if you think you're getting away with your crimes without punishment, *Prince.*"

I reach for my dagger hidden under my cloak, but alcohol is not my friend tonight. An ice encased fist connects with my jaw and sends me flying into a burly patron behind me. Within seconds, brawls and shattered glass fill the room. I struggle to my feet and find myself in the cross hairs of the bard. With a devilish grin he straps his lute to his back, then extends an open palm towards me. An orb of flaming blue builds, and I can do nothing but watch the fatal beauty before me.

Then, his white fluffed ears perk, as if hearing a shout obvious only to him. With a primal snarl, his orb of Aether disappears. "This isn't over, Prince!" He shouts, then disappears into thin air, an echoing crack snapping through the tavern. Screams rip behind me and I turn my head to face sentries shooting civilians with the tainted arrows Orion and I made, the ones Father assured were not to be used on our own people.

The ones intended to give it's victim a torturous demise that lasts for four days, on the third day recovery seems possible and brings hope, but the last day squeezes blood from every pore. Easy to determine traitors and display their consequences to all, as Typhan says.

I have no choice, I can't be caught here. I focus all my Aether in my mind's eye on the only place I've ever felt safe, hoping I have enough magic left to get me there. As I crawl into the Aether hole I've opened I glance back, and really wish I hadn't.

Onya is draped over the bar, her lifeless eyes staring at the ceiling as guards surround her body with malicious intent in their sick eyes.

21

Find the poet.

I land in a heap on Lone Island, which is nothing more than a bedroom sized flat rock rising precious feet from the murky depths. A storm is brewing in the north and churns the water around me, splashing cold onto my refuge centered in the lake. I vomit shame, alcohol and bile all over myself, the rock and into the water.

Once the minutes long heaves have turned dry and no longer wrack my body, I lay on my side and curl my knees into my chest. I linger on the stone's edge and fall apart, hot tears mingling with mist and familiar siren songs. Their melody rises and I fall into a trance, their peaceful voices aid in my morning meditation and usually grant me solitude. Not tonight, though. Tonight, I am caught in the cyclical hurricane of my own self hatred.

Murderer.

Monster.

Kidnapper.

Villain.

I am every bit my Father, molded into the perfect killer, just the way he intended. Orion tugs on the bond from a distance and waits for my answer. With great difficulty I sit up just enough to evaluate the distant lake sides, but I can't see past through the moonless night and past choppy waters. Typhan's threat weighs heavy on my shoulders and the thought of a world without Orion, or my mother, is too much to bear.

No, I cannot strike down my own.

White vines of Aether keep Orion and I imprisoned on our knees, two children forced to watch their Father execute his delightful torture. Water drips from the cavernous ceiling into a diluted puddle of blood on the broken stone between my brother and I. Orion's scrawny teenage body struggles against his bonds, but I had given up minutes ago.

"I will ask you once more, Yira, where is the tunnel?" Typhan asks our mother sweetly, curling her beautiful hair around his crimson fingers. His chest is bare and his neatly pressed black dress pants are speckled with her blood. Mother's arms and legs are bound by chains cutting into her skin, naked body stretched out on a vertical wooden table. She stares at Typhan with a cracked silent grin, despite her state, and ours.

"Just tell him Mother!" Orion screams.

"Orion, quiet!" I give him a harsh glare and snarl. Father won't hesitate twice to kill him too, the sick male's plan for when I come of age is the only thing keeping Orion alive. A plan I will never partake in, though I have to entertain the thought if I want to keep my brother alive long enough to get us out of here.

Typhan straightens and releases her matted locks from his fingers, then paces across the dungeon and kneels before Orion and I. He rubs his scruffed chin and looks back and forth between his shaking sons, then his white eyes alight with a terrible idea. Dread fills my soul and I inadvertently twist under his searing white vines of restraining Aether.

*Typhan delicately caresses one of the imprisoning tendrils of white surrounding me, then rises, clasping his hands together. "I have a wonderful idea, one that will surely keep our **family** from unraveling any further!" He bounds over to Mother and whispers into her ear, finally causing horror to* spread across her face.

"This can't be good." Orion relays over the bond to me.

"Just do as he says, we just have to get Mother out of here and get to the break in the Wall."

"Don't you get it? We're never getting out of here, Al." Orion's usual uncertainty is replaced by pure, dread filled confidence. When my mother nods, her eyes closed and body weighed with defeat, his words sink in. Typhan's Aether bonds constrict tighter around both of us, and I fight with every bit of my being as air is pushed from my lungs. Tendrils of white sweep around Typhan, and Mother.

"Stop it!" I shout, immature Aether sparking in my veins. I'm only a few months off from my magic finally coming to life, but it's too late. Mother's eyes remain closed, even as Orion lets out a howl. Pain flows through me just as Aether and blood does, but I scowl at Typhan's satisfied grin. A blade unsheathes from his side, reflecting the glowing white magic illuminating the dank cell. He snaps his fingers and a metal bowl appears in his other hand.

First, he makes a shallow slice under Mother's breast which draws a flinch from her, then scrapes his blade across the edge of the bowl, allowing every drop of blood to trickle in. He slices his own shoulder as he approaches me, adding his oily blood to Mother's in the same fashion. He kneels before me and caresses my cheek tenderly with a devilish smile, but I spit in his face.

"Go to hell."

Typhan laughs, the skin crawling sound deafening. He harshly slices down the left side of my face, blinding pain twists with a hollow scream caught in my throat. Orion cries when the pain travels down the bond seconds later than I experience it. I cannot move as the bowl rests under my chin, a steady flow of warmth trailing down my face into it, more of my blood filling the bowl than anyone else's thus far.

"We're already there."

I can't see out of my left eye, whether it's from the river of blood or because my vision is damaged I can't tell, but I can see Typhan kneel before Orion at *my right. I close my eyes and swiftly switch bodies with Orion, giving him no choice. Something we've only done once, and it didn't last long before.*

I keep my, or Orion's eyes rather, closed, or else Typhan will see the color flash as I kick Orion out of his body. His thick hand wraps around my weak throat and tightens as the blade tickles underneath my right pointed ear. "You're lucky I find you useful, or else I would do more than tickle you with this knife." He whispers into my other ear, though his message is intended for Orion.

I will the thin body to shake in usual Orion fashion and nod once with eyes still shut tight, then the blade kisses my palm with a searing bite. Typhan's footsteps retreat and Orion yanks me out of his body, and I slam into mine. I hunch against the still fervent bonds and shake dizziness from my head, slinging blood. I remember my injury and my throbbing headache intensifies into a swelling hurricane, left eye the center of my pain.

"What did you do that for!" Orion chides through the bond.

"I didn't want you to feel it." I say simply.

"You're an idiot, Alvis."

"You're welcome." I chirp, attempting to remain light, even as Typhan swirls our family's blood together with his knife tip.

"From this day forth, and until the day each of us die, we shall be bound by blood. Orion and Alvis cannot conspire to harm me in any fashion, or do so physically or by means of Aether. They cannot leave the walls of Silverbury unless I say so." Typhan orders, his command tightening the Aether chains until they dig into my skin.

No, no. This can't be happening.

"Furthermore, Yira shall be physically or verbally unable to organize any more of these foolish rebel groups, or smuggle any more Fae or Humans out of Sylvan." A soft cry emits from Mother and she finally locks tear filled eyes with Orion and I, desperate violet searching us for forgiveness. We've known about her 'crimes', but they do not shame us. She has finally given up after centuries of fighting, that is where her guilt lies.

I wish I could tell her to feel no such thing.

*"And one more thing," Typhan keeps his gaze on me, a smile playing at his lips, "You two, Orion and Alvis, will not be able to resist a command or order given by **me**, my word will be law. Dutiful sons, shall we say?"*

"It's servitude!" Orion barks, fighting against the vines that are now almost entirely immersed into his skin, and all of ours. Typhan smirks, evil flaring in his hard set white eyes.

*"The blood bond **can** be broken if ... " Typhan holds up a finger and I narrow my brows, the whole point of a blood bond is that they **can't** be broken.*

*"Hmm, let's see, for example, dear Alvis, if you decide to disobey my command, a horrific and tortuous death would befall your Mother **and** Orion. Attempted assassination or conspiracy will earn you the death of her, and Orion. However, if either of you plan to escape or succeed, only your Mother will receive a fatal fate." Elation fills his last statement, and I stare at him with stunned fury. He wants us to betray her, otherwise he wouldn't word the condition in such a way.*

*"And dear Yira, if you break your bond or **ever** attempt to leave me again," Typhan grasps her chin firmly and pulls her face upwards, chains clinking as his smile fades into a snarl. "**Both** of your sons shall die, and your soul shall be bound to **mine**, for all of our eternal life."*

"And you? You have no conditions?" I ask, tears falling without apology. Typhan smiles wide and tilts his head.

*"I am not the traitor here, Alvis. Even thinking about killing me will you set you ablaze, as it **should**." With an echoing crackle and resounding snap, the vines sink into all of us, our blood bond permanently marked for all eternity, or until one of us breaks.*

I slip into the icy water and command the lazy molecules to crowd my lungs and take me to the bottom. Sirens surround me, a beautiful rainbow composed of hundreds of merfae pleading with me in another language I will never understand, though I'm sure they're begging me to surface. High Fae are so afraid of the tempting beings, though they only drown those who are dishonest. Which in Sylvan, are quite a few.

I close my eyes and fight the pressure in my chest, ignoring the desperate calls I will not heed even if I could understand. Orion and I befriended many as children and freed merfae from the mariner's nets too many times to count. Sandy bottom and childhood memories ground me as all labels fade away. I am no one here, and nothing can hurt me. Orion will live and become High Lord, Mother will live. *Zemer* and hundreds of others like him will have their vengeance.

"But what about you, dear Alvis?" Crooning disturbs my peace and my drowning spirit is saved, a bubble of air surrounding my heaving body in an instant. I sputter out water and slam my fists into the sand.

"Why! Just leave me *be!*" I sob into my hands for a strangled minute, then lock eyes with the being who stopped me. A pink and white striped feminine body draped in layers of translucent jellyfish like appendages, with an exquisite iridescent mertail that tapers to a fatally sharp point. Piercing pink eyes flash with delight, she swims around the generous air bubble casually, then halts before me. She studies me through the shield and knits her webbed fingers, then gives me a sly smile.

"I didn't raise the shield, child. I merely asked a question, which was one you desperately needed to hear." She riddles in the Fae tongue, her voice deeper than the sirens and her figure twice the size as well. Kelp trails from her petite head and floats about her wide waist. My heart jumps and I open my trembling lips, but nothing comes out.

This must be an Ancient.

"What, what do you mean, you're saying that this," I gesture to the air bubble, "this is me?" I stutter as sea life meanders by the orb as if I'm just a rock in their way.

The sandy bottom is gorgeous, plant life and glimmering conch shells the size of my head are illuminated by luminescent cities of coral reefs. Plants reminiscent of trees with 'bark' far more textured than their tropical counterparts above ground. I have to tilt my head back to find the top of one, the broad leaves reminding me of the Ancient's hair. In the murky distance across the sea floor an array of lights can be seen, but I cannot discern any shapes.

The sight makes me realize just how deep the lake is, and reminds me that no one has ever reached bottom before, and returned alive, that is. A flash of rose magic from the Ancient's eyes draws my attention back to her patient figure, and I find myself afraid. "You manipulate water in ways our kind has never seen before. You have a destiny waiting for you, and it's not with your father." She explains, soft voice haunting me.

"That's impossible, you know what these mean." I shake my head, body trembling as I rise from the sand. I gesture to my tattoos, then glance up to the distant Lone Island. The bond between Orion and I is oddly silent, it's only a matter of moments before he travels there and tries to save me.

"No matter what I do, someone dies. I don't want to hurt people anymore." I exhale, and my shoulders drop.

"People die every day, child, this is nothing new. Leave this place at once, and return only when you have the weapon you can not wield. Your dear Mother is tired of being his leverage, and has asked me to push you along."

"How do you know what my Mother wants?" I snap, voice cracking as I march closer to the shield between us, tears choking my fury. It's true, Mother has begged me over the years to take Orion and go before I'm ordered to kill him, but I cannot bring myself to plan her death anymore than I can his.

"Water is always listening, and always ready to share." She replies, vertical pupils dilating before her pink eyes flare so bright I have to shield my vision.

"Find the weapon you can not wield, He shall reign, and you shall walk with the poet who becomes a king. Brace for the fall, and never falter, dear child." Her booming voice shatters through my body and I drop to my knees, her command and prophecy burning a hole into my twisted mind.

"I don't know what any of that means!"

Sinister laughs echoes as the bubble collapses inwards and my body is thrust to the surface. I cling to the side of Lone island and cough up glacial water, barely able to hang on as my body shuts down. The Ancient's pink eyes and kelp hair surfaces, and her last words haunt me the most. "Find the poet."

Orion drops onto the island from an Aether hole as she disappears, his violet eyes wildly find me struggling to stay afloat. "Al!" He pulls me out of the water and settles on the rock with my frozen body in his arms, rocking me back and forth.

"I'm fine, always so dramatic." I attempt to joke, but end up coughing blood up on the chemical ridden tunic I found him in earlier.

"What in the hell were you doing!" Orion shakes me and I release a deep sigh, then fully open the bond between us, silently offering him all the answers. Orion stares blankly over the lake and lives through my recent memories, then focuses on me with horror. Tears roll from under his misted glasses and he looks as if he can't decide whether to hit me, or hold me. "You were going to leave me?"

"I can't live without you or take you away from this world, you've always been the best of us." I whisper, letting more honesty out then I originally intended. "Typhan has wanted this before the blood bond was even made, and I could never kill you. Or Mother."

I break into my brother's chest once more, more tears have fallen tonight than in my entire life. "Oh Alvis," Orion sobs and we hold onto each other for dear life, "You and me, that's how we live."

Well, that's a dumb question.

Seagulls usher in the new day and carry on incessantly outside the open air dining hall on their way to the lake below, and for a moment I envy them. I run a hand through my clean locks, the freshly trimmed sides scratch against my palm. Fresh air cuts through the lofty hall decorated with towering crystalline pillars and granite floors. Gemstones and gold are littered everywhere our grand banquet of food is not, and the luminous sun reflects a rainbow from the fine cuts of crystal across the vaulted ceiling.

"Alvis, did you hear me?" I snap out of my stupor and focus on Typhan at the other end of the long wooden table detailed with sapphires, then straighten casually in my seat.

"He wants to know if you heard about the Shipwreck collapsing." Orion clues me in through the bond and I avoid looking at him, stretching my leathered arms overhead and hardly missing another beat.

"Oh yes, some *mysterious* fellow bought the place out and partied too hard, as I understand it." I grin wide and pay no attention to Mother who is beaming in the seat to Father's right, like nothing is wrong, like the dutiful wife she is bound to be. She is dressed in a fine purple silk dress, modestly cut and sleeveless. Thick gold necklaces from Typhan

30

adorn her neck, and matching cuffs rest on her high pointed ears.

Apollo and I are the only ones dressed in full fighting leathers and an arsenal of weapons, our usual attire on days like today. Collection Day, when we leave the city walls in search of Fae to enslave and experiment on. Since the day Vabel burned, only he and I go on these missions now.

"Well, dear son, *I* heard you had something to do with that." Typhan taunts, giving me a knowing smile. I press a hand to my chest and scoff, earning a snort from Orion to my right. He's dressed in plain silver and teal linen tunic and trousers for his scheduled day in the library, his adventuring clothes hidden in the lab. Our entire lives our days have been planned for us, making today's escapade tricky.

Apollo grumbles something about my being a drunk in the seat to my left, but I ignore his sullen features. Out of all us he should be the one jumping for joy, he loves going on 'hunts', as he calls them. After closer inspection of the purple lining the fair skin under his white eyes and crimson staining his chipped fingernails, I realize he's already had a long morning.

"Now Father, I may be known to drink from time to time, but I would *never* break the place! Truly was my favorite, what a shame."

"Well nonetheless, the *fellow* was caught last night, and won't budge." Typhan raises a thick brow and strokes his dreaded beard, then leans back in his chair. He gestures for Mother to sit in his lap and she obliges, eating a grape as she does so. He snakes a hand around her wide waist, keeping me in his gaze as she feeds him one of the red globes.

Mother's eyes flash with a subtleness only I recognize, confirming my suspicion that this *Zemer* is tied to *her* Captain. If he does break, she will be the one to pay for it.

"Well, I suppose after Apollo has a turn I'll give it a go, I did hear something about a fresh ship in town last night. I planned on doing some investigating this morning, looks like you saved me the trouble."

"I already spent the night listening to that brat yap about everything *but* what we need." Apollo grunts, shoving his untouched plate back and crossing his black leathered arms. Apollo is notoriously bloodthirsty, for anyone to make it through his torture and not break is a feat.

"I do hope I have, saved you the trouble, that is." Typhan wonders aloud with a primal tone, a half smile present on his face. Mother's smile falters as his fingers press too hard into her abdomen, and she caresses his arm as I corral my anger.

"I'm sure Alvis will sort it all out, you did appoint him your lead scoutmaster for a reason, and you're never wrong, my dear." She assures Father in a murmur. Typhan's hand loosens and his eyes brighten as he pulls out of his bloodthirsty trance, then he waves me off.

"Find out who he's working for, then get rid of him." I rise and leave my own food untouched, giving my Father an obligatory show of respect before leaving by thrumming my fist to my chest. He ignores me and proceeds to harass Apollo about his failing new group of recruits.

"You know what to do." I tell Orion.

On my way out, I can't help but smile.

What a vague command, I've become quite good at finding holes in Faerie deals, just like my Mother.

* * *

I stand in the center dungeon aisle, glaring at a closed solid iron door which holds the *Zemer* on the other side. Fists tighten and my eye twitches, blood roars in my ears. No matter how hard I try, all I see is that dreaded night so many years ago, the beginning of actual hell. Dim scones line the stone underbelly of the castle and rows upon rows of cells fill the silent dungeon.

Two steel plated guards stand in silence at either end of each row, and each row holds fifty cells. There are twenty rows of cells and Interrogation rooms on this level, though the cavernous space is small compared to what the Doorway of Death holds in the lab above. I am down here nearly every day, usually to interrogate Fae deemed traitors or spies by Typhan, but never this room. Father must not be happy with how I reacted last night in the throne room and I have a feeling soon his request will become an order, then I cannot disobey.

Orion approaches my side with caution and rests a hand on my tense shoulder. *"It's just a room."* He offers over the bond and I nod, then my hands loosen. I give him a smile and pull my mask of strength back on, pressing my forehead to his before he leaves me.

"You're sure this is going to work?" I ask Orion as he paces away to the end of this row in search of the spiral staircase waiting in a different section, the steps lead to his Aether Lab on the level above in this underground labyrinth.

"I hope so."

With that, he leaves to resume his regularly scheduled programming in the library, and I enter the interrogation cell where I was forced into a lifelong blood bond with my entire family two centuries ago. An olive skinned Fire Fae servant huddles in the farthest corner, his orange eyes aglow with sparking Aether and heating the small room to beyond bearable. I halt before the same table my mother was once tortured on and cross my arms, then attempt to determine how this male is still alive.

Blood covers every bit of his naked body of course, the table is not only vertical but inclined forward so his lacerated body hangs only by the chains around his wrists, the ones around his feet slack. He doesn't dangle lifelessly though, his entire torso and arms strain as he attempts to relieve some of the weight. After a moment he lifts his head, blonde hair matted with oil and blood, crisped and scalped in some places. His swollen bloodshot eyes flash blue, just as defiant as last night, and he smiles with a wide cracked grin.

"Took you long enough." He spits out, voice hoarse and blood dribbling down his chin. Gushing lacerations have mutilated his softly angled freckled face, they litter the rest of his body as well but I attempt to give him some dignity and keep my eyes trained on his smile.

"Well, I'm sure my Father would've indulged you if you asked for a *specific* tormentor." I drawl while searching his face for fear, though I find none. A half smile fills my own face and I chuckle. "You're a tough bastard, I'll give you that."

"Have to be when you're hunted your entire life." He retorts, choking on his words and something else. I will myself to remain still when he spits out fountain of blood, and a tooth. "Finally, been trying to get that out for *ages.*"

"Why are you here?" I ask with curiosity, my hand resting on the iron crank at the side of the table. He glances sideways to me and winces, much to his chagrin, the entire right side of his face is swollen immensely.

"Well, that's a dumb question isn't it?" I blink and tilt my head, waiting until he continues. "I told you, I'm here for your head. Cap has different ideas but," He trails off, muttering, and I slowly turn the crank until the blood soaked wooden table creaks back to horizontal.

With a careful finger I hover over the gashes across his wrists and face, he scowls and yanks his face away. I smirk and conjure a storm cloud in my hand, which draws his wide eyed attention back to me. The short Fire Fae male shakily stands in his corner, awestruck by my Aether. The sight of the *Zemer* made me forget about him. I jut my chin to the door and he scurries into action, taking his sweltering heat with him.

"Wait." I order in a gentle tone, paralyzing the filthy ginger haired male with his hand on the door. Same as Air Fae replace poison with fresh air, Fire Fae replace cold with warmth, in this case overbearing warmth, all the while they slowly freeze to death.

I pace over to him, unsnapping my cloak from my leathered shoulders as I do. I sling it across his skeletal frame and stare down at his wonderfully confused face with indifference. I narrow my brows and pin the encompassing sapphire blue fabric together over his chest with the pin Typhan gave me years ago, a golden sword. I lean forward, hands clasped behind my back, and whisper in the trembling Fire Fae's ginger fluffed ear.

"The fabric alone is worth more than your life, I suggest you get rid of it, quickly."

On the last snarling word I shove the dumbstruck Fae out the door, then straighten my leathers before turning back to the storm cloud which now encompasses the table. *Zemer's* chest heaves, eyes locked onto the brewing darkness above him, then his attention snaps on me when I stand by his side once more. I keep my hands clasped tight behind my back and stare down at him with the arrogant mask of the Prince.

"Well this is a new one, what'll you do, zap me to death?" *Zemer* snarks and I chuckle darkly, resisting the heart wrenching urge to brush filthy hair from his wild eyes. I had a feeling he was in league with this Captain, and if what he says is true, I don't foresee him betraying their orders, as much as he'd like to.

I blow on the cloud and it spirals over his restrained body, increasing further in size as it darkens to near black. Thick condensation presses against dungeon walls now icing over without the Fire Fae's magic, mixing with the stench of death stuck onto every stone in the oppressive room. "If I take the cuffs off, what will you do?" I muse, tracing the metal chains lining his wrists with a light gloved finger.

"*Definitely* take a solid piss, you know how long I've been waiting to do that? Isn't quite the same when you can't aim." He sighs with gentle exasperation whilst staring at the ceiling, as if he just described

35

paradise.

"Just *how* have you managed it thus far? You're so mouthy ..." I quip, then my brow furrows when he winces mid wicked smile. Blood further pools on the table beneath him from his extensive latticework of injuries, Apollo's work no doubt. He plays with blades, and Father plays with minds. I do both quite well, but not today.

"I've heard the Prince of Whores and his kin likes that kind of thing, mouthiness and all." He jabs, and I cannot hide the furious surprise that overcomes me.

"Always believe everything you hear?" I ask with cold seriousness, then snap my fingers which unlocks the cuffs with a reverberating click. A delicious groan escapes the *Zemer* and he gingerly lowers his arms, resting them at his side while he stares at the enlarged storm cloud with wonder, not fear.

I turn away whilst gentle rain patters onto his freckled skin, washing away all blood and wounds from his body, head to toe. I walk over to a rickety small table opposite the room and retrieve his washed clothes from last night, folded with care. Images of Father folding Mother's clothes before torturing her sends a shudder through me. Exhaustion suddenly overtakes me while my magic finishes it's work, I underestimated how intense his injuries were.

I grip the edge of the table for a moment, my other hand rubs at a pounding headache settling in my right temple. After burying the sudden exhaustion and pain, I face the now sitting up male and keep my gaze on his now clean and healed face, satisfaction flowing through me from studying my handiwork. Water Fae are the only kind who can heal, and I am one of the best.

When I'm not causing bodily harm, that is.

He waits with crossed arms and I hand him his clothes, then step backwards and wait with hands clasped behind my back, eyes locked onto his own blazing sapphires. He is unlike any Water Fae I've encountered before, and the memory of his ice encased fist from last night, not to mention the icy blue flame magic, piques my curiosity. Patches of missing curled blonde hair weren't replaced by my healing storm, but he's still fascinating to me all the same.

"What, have to start with a clean slate before you torture me?" *Zemer* remarks, a light brow raised as he catches me staring.

"Get dressed." I order, then avert my eyes when he jumps up at once and pulls on his pants. A chuckle emits from the male as he stands, bare chested and full of energy.

"Where are we going? What are we doing? On a scale of 1-10 right now, how tired are you from wasting your magic on me?" He speaks so quick my head spins in a circle and I stumble forwards, placing a hand over his mouth.

"Shut up for *two* seconds, I have a plan and it involves you being quiet." I whisper harshly, he yanks back from my touch and scowls.

"A *plan?*" He demands in a conspicuous manner, throwing the sandy short sleeved tunic over his head.

"What did I literally *just* say?" I throw my arms up as I walk to the door.

"Wait, I'm not dressed yet!" He yells in a whisper, then topples over whilst pulling on the boots I forgot under the table. He springs across the room and slams into me waiting at the exit, then shakes his head fervently. "Does this mean she convinced you?"

"Who?" I ask, concentration and patience broken. He opens his lips but gurgling voices bellow from the dungeon and we both freeze. It's time. I glare down at him and he returns the scowl. After the voices pass I pinch the bridge of my nose and sigh. "If you want to get out of here, then do *exactly* as I say. We'll talk about who, and why later."

He opens his lips to protest and his brows furrow so tight I have to keep from laughing. After a long moment, he pushes out a heavy breath. "Fine."

With that, I open the door and we step into the first hallway of endless cells. I gesture for him to follow me, and sleeping guards now litter the dim tunnels along the way. Orion slipped a concoction into the drinks he brought before I arrived and used ingredients that would take effect well *after* I entered the cell, and it worked well by the looks. There are still so many moving parts, dread fills me the more I think about it. It's inevitable for a quickly put together plan to have a weak point, and I anticipate it around every corner we turn in silence.

To his credit, I nearly forget the light footed bard shadowing my every move. When I come to the top of the spiral staircase and peer both ways down the empty stone tunnel, I sprint for the Lab door. I turn the handle and *Zemer* shudders behind me. Anyone with a sense of decency would, the scent of decay and chemicals splashes across you the moment you stand outside it.

We enter the dark lab, empty and with the Doorway to Death ajar. I retrieve my pack, tucked into a cupboard in the far and cleaned up dissection area. Orion's gear is gone, that's a good sign. In my hurry I don't notice the horrified male evaluating the organ specimens in jars and poisonous plants littering the room.

"What is this place?" He asks in a whisper, halting my steps. My fists tighten as he searches my eyes from across the room, his own alight with a soft blue flame.

"Let's go." I march for the mortuary door and my hand pauses on the iron knob, a deep breath stuck in my chest. I glance over my shoulder to *Zemer*, my shoulders curling in. "I apologize in advance for what you are about to see, and I mean it when I say I hope one day I can explain." *Zemer* gives me a curt nod, then we step inside.

Glass cylinders encased in a copper framework stretch from floor to lofty ceiling and line the bright stone hall, each filled with a light green preserving liquid and a bloated body. Hundreds of cylinders situated in rows fill the expanse, lining the center walkway. Tubes and hoses protrude from each fifteen foot tall cylinder, and dead bodies stare lifelessly from every angle of the endless place. I straighten my shoulders and keep my eyes on the empty cylinder at the far end, beside the one Orion filled yesterday. Even after death Typhan demands we keep the bodies, just in case they prove useful.

I swallow upon seeing the face of the female Orion has spent months injecting Aether into, her once beautiful skin bloated with green preserving fluid. Tormented bright purple eyes stare out, and I find myself stuck in her judgmental stare from beyond the grave. Long black hair floats around her young naked body like a cloak of death, and my heart beats wildly out of my chest as movement twitches in her fingers. I take a step closer to the cylinder and reach a shaking hand out to the thick glass, panic fills me further as another twitch jolts her entire arm. Am I going crazy?

Zemer searches the cylinders frantically and his voice cracks so loud I stop in my tracks, my white vined hand inches away from the thick heated glass. *"No …"* I turn on my heel and find his trembling hand reaching out for a chamber two rows deep from the walkway, his eyes filled with tears. Shame heats my neck, the dead human inside is one I recognize well. The night all hell broke loose in Vabel, he was one of the first villagers to fight back after Loyska, the leader and deadliest of the *Nafshyi,* showed our hand.

I don't remember this *Zemer* being there though. Suddenly the handsome male is before me, clenching the leathers tight across my chest. I stare down at him and grind my jaw, waiting patiently for him to hit me. Instead, his softly angled face crumples and tears stream further down his reddened cheeks.

"Why?"

"I had no choice." I say earnestly, searching his flaming oceanic eyes. Air catches in his lungs as he evaluates me. He must find something redeeming, as he releases me and takes shaky steps back. Voices echo from the Lab beyond, the inevitable weak spot in our plan. I sprint to the empty chamber at the end and climb in, then gesture for him to follow suit.

"You've *got* to be kidding me." *Zemer snaps*, wary of stepping inside a device his friend is floating in just a few feet away.

"You have to trust me." Shouts turn fearsome and he glances at the far entrance to the lab, then back to me with doubt filling his eyes. "Trust me."

As voices threaten to catch us, he wordlessly jumps in beside me, and I tell myself he doesn't trust me, just has no other choice.

"Hold on tight." I warn, then flick a switch on the inside wall of the chamber. The metal plate beneath our feet disappears, and we free fall into a spiraling tunnel. *Zemer* yelps and clings to me, and I laugh heartily in a fit of hysteria. "Hope you don't mind getting your feet wet!"

Light approaches, my temporary joy muffled by rushing air. Our tunnel drops us at the bottom of the castle overhanging the lake, into choppy water below. After orienting myself I dive further into the depths and gesture for a confused *Zemer* to follow. We circle the craggy rock shelf the grand castle above rests on. After yesterday's underwater antics, my lungs struggle after only a minute of searching.

Luckily, the familiar narrow passage hidden in the rock side makes itself known with a flash of purple, and we swim into the narrow tunnel. After several feet, a near translucent lilac shield blankets the awaiting entrance. I still haven't learned who built the tunnel after all this time, or cast the shield, but I know it would be in violation of the bond for Mother to do so directly. Perhaps the Ancients really have been on her side, in a sick way.

Once we pass through the humming shield the water level drops dramatically and our tunnel empties into a wide cavern. Waiting on the rocky shoreline is Orion and Mother, the four shivering Air Fae children from the Lab, and an unfamiliar tall female in a feathered hat. Upon seeing my family, energy replaces exhaustion and I rush out of the water, straight into Orion's arms.

"You made it." We say at the same time, embracing the other tight.

"You brought them." I say, glancing to the three trembling children clinging to the rosy haired eldest.

"I couldn't leave them behind, they would've been first in Apollo's path." Orion replies, brushing off the deed. I pull back after a moment and rest a hand on Mother's shoulder, returning her soft smile. *Zemer* is fiercely debating with the raven haired female near the entrance to another tunnel, our exit. I haven't been down here since before the blood bond was made, but it hasn't changed a bit.

I glance at the arguing pair and wonder just *how* Mother has been smuggling after all this time, and if this these two have been working with her longer than I thought. "You must go now, he will be here any minute." Mother pleads with quiet tears in her flashing violet eyes, sadness tainting her full smile.

"Are you sure this is what you want?" Orion asks as he hugs her, her soft body dressed in soaked purple silks folds into his easily. I wrap my arms around both of them, the words from the Ancient stirring in my mind. The children are waiting at the tunnel with the others, and suddenly my oddly calm heart begins racing.

"Yes," She inhales a deep breath, her voice filled with peace, "I cannot watch you two live like this anymore. You are my pride, and how my work lives on. Don't ever stop fighting, do you hear?"

"Never falter." I whisper, and Orion repeats my sentiment. A quake shakes the cavern and I hold my family as rocks crash beside us and into the water. Screams cut through the air from the children, echoing off through the cavern. A multitude of six foot long glowing white talons emerge from the tunnel we swum through. Magic claws through rock like it's butter, and a deafening roar fills the chasm as the lilac shield snaps. Air catches in my paralyzed chest at the sight, and *Zemer* shoves my shoulder.

"We need to go!" He shouts, breaking me from my trance. I glance back down to Mother, then Orion. My brother and I hug our Mother one last time, then we run after *Zemer* and his companion to the uphill exit. I am the last to enter and an explosion shakes the chasm behind me. I am thrown forwards and my skull connects with stone, hands scrape as dizziness settles at once.

Orion howls in the distance in response to my pain and shouts float above from every direction. I sit up too fast and darkness takes over further. Strong hands slide under my torso and legs, my vision returns after a long moment to find Orion carrying me. I glance back to the chaos left behind and hot tears stream down my face at the sight.

Typhan stands at the entrance to our escape tunnel, glowing white eyes alighting his devious smile and darkness surrounding him. Mother is at his side, and a possessive hand rests on her shoulder.

Despite her impending doom, she is smiling.

I promise it's worth it.

∽ᴏᴐᴏᴐᴏ

Minutes turn to hours, and nothing but silence keeps us company on our winding journey to the surface. The female leading us follows a small floating fire orb, and I trail behind the group with Orion ahead of me. After the initial shock I regained enough energy to walk, but not much more. All I can do is dwell on what happens once we are officially past the walls, and Orion has been thinking the same as well.

I catch the *Zemer* glancing back at me now and then with a hard expression shadowed by the dim orb ahead of him, but I mostly focus my attention on the slate ground reflecting the flickering fire and not falling. The farther we travel, the more intense Orion and I's encasing vine tattoos burn across our bodies.

"We're almost there, do you feel it?" Orion asks, inner voice shaky and full of pain.

"Yes ..." I manage, stumbling over a stone and nearly falling into him. *"You and me, that's how we live, right?"*

"That's how we live, and never falter." Orion reiterates as we walk side by side, his arm looping through mine when I stumble once more.

A small tug quirks one side of my lips up, but faint moonlight streaming in at the end of the tunnel wipes my face clean. *Zemer* waits with a smile outside the exit with his companion and the children, but Orion and I are forced to stop. Crisp air and moonlight is within inches from my soaked boots before Orion and I drop to our knees in anguish, a primal growl rips my chest in two.

Orion whimpers as he clutches his side and I want to tear my leg off, the vines along my left thigh the most constricting and painful. Every inch of our matching tattoos flare through clothing, blinding me within seconds. *Zemer* rushes to my side and I snarl, unable to push him away or warn him through the searing agony. He takes my now bare bicep and his fingers sizzle at once, but no cry leaves him.

"What's happening to them!" He wildly focuses on his female companion surrounded by crying children, gesturing to Orion and I with what looks like panic in his sparking blue eyes. I shake my head but it's no use, dizziness rattles my senses furthers. Even through the mind numbing pain hugging every limb, one crystal clear question floats through my mind.

Is he really worried?

"This is the extent of their bond, another step takes them officially out of Silverbury," The Fire Fae's somber voice pauses as the orb dims, grief filling her porcelain face as she focuses on me, "I promise I'll make it worth it, to take the next step."

I rise with great difficulty and extend a hand to Orion, pulling him up with *Zemer's* assistance much to my dismay. The fair Fae grimaces whilst holding up Orion's other side, silently enduring the heat ruminating from Orion's bonds as we walk out of the tunnel together. Excruciating pain swells to crescendo and I almost fall into oblivion, but the Fire Fae is at my side before I fall forwards. Flashes of Mother in the chasm slash my mind, images of Typhan's hands around her neck choke my spirit and air is difficult to find.

Zemer and his companion start off by holding Orion and I up, but by the time we fully pass into wheat grass they are dragging our writhing bodies. Burning flesh fills the night and my vision leaves entirely, despite feeling unfamiliar grass for the first time in ages, my heart breaks.

A solid crack of vertebrae fills the air and I scream harmoniously with Mother, suffering underground at the hands of a monster. Orion screams in tune and our bonds burn with a new intensity as her life flickers in the distance. *Zemer* cries out and drops Orion, the impact jolting my own body.

The female must've anticipated it, her slim body stiffens before I fall out of her arms. She gingerly lays me down and shouts at the bard, her jumbled words muffled by a high frequency humming. I reach out with a charred hand, feeling for Orion in the grass beside me fading in and out of consciousness. Another reverberating snap folds my ears down and I cry out, a flash of Mother's femur snapped in two burns into my memory.

He's literally breaking her, piece by piece.

Crisp winter air replaces the stench of flesh melting away and as the world fades, so does the pain. A soft voice coos from above and I smile, his words and a rushing wind sending me off. "Don't go anywhere, you're gonna be okay, I promise. Hey, **don't** go anywhere."

* * *

Intense sunlight strikes my face and I sigh, nestling further under thick furs. Comfort swallows my tired body whole, but is quickly followed by heart stopping panic. Confusion draws my brows together and I jolt upwards with a dizzying start.

An entire home is neatly packed into the small space, warm colored decking composes the floor, walls and ceiling. The space is mostly a study, a grand mahogany desk commands the room and giant bay windows reveal the world behind the high backed seat. Fluffed clouds meander by and a vented window invites a breeze which flutters parchment along the desk, and my brother's hair on the pillow beside me. His peaceful face holds no fear, no worries or distrust, and the sight brings a smile to my dry lips.

Memories of last night's terror return to me and my smile is replaced by a tight grimace. I roll over in the unfamiliar bed to evaluate the rest of the room, only to find the raven haired female from last night perched on a wooden stool beside me. I reach under the pillow out of habit and find a blade, but it's not mine. I tighten my grip on the stout dagger and sit up, flickering Aether coursing through my still tired body.

"Seems you have the same habits as a pirate after all, dear Prince." She brushes dirt off the feathered oil skin hat in her lap and raises an arching black brow at me, a soft smile apparent as she teases.

"Where are we?" I ask gruffly, eyes narrowed on the porcelain Fire Fae. Her appearance is quite jolting, crimson eyes illuminate her near translucent skin and contrast her lengthy dark hair. She's dressed in garb similar to before, a leather militia jacket covering a plain white modestly laced tunic and layers of leather belts. She's nothing like any Fire Fae I've seen, then again I've only encountered Fire Fae as slaves.

"Nearly to Farhaven, I believe." She sighs and rubs her forehead, then the Aether in her eyes flare as she focuses on me once more. My heart leaps in my chest at the intensity and I focus my breathing when Orion stirs beside me, I don't want to wake him. She chuckles lightly and returns the hat upon her head. "No worries Prince, I made a vow to your Mother to keep you safe whilst on my ship, given you agree to my terms."

"How did she even plan this? The bond ... " I trail off, realizing how severe the burns are across my body, eyes first catching the blistered vines along my thick arms. Heat rushes my cheeks when I realize I'm bare chested in a female's presence, but she doesn't seem to be interested. Fine by me.

"I will be brutally honest with you, Alvis, is it?" She asks and I nod, jaw tightening. "I've been in the business a long time, made a lot of connections. When they started disappearing, I started looking. See where I'm going with this?"

I nod once more and swallow the burning shame rising in my throat. A realization hits me and I laugh suddenly. "You're the pirates Typhan has been chasing his tail over, fighting for the royalty who can't be bothered to get off their ass."

She smiles and leans forward, her expression darkening. "I don't fight for the royalty, I fight for the people, but you are correct. However, you know what really kicked me into gear?" I shake my head, biting my cheek. "Vabel."

"I don't remember you there, or," I hurriedly say, but realize I still don't know *Zemer's* actual name. The female watches me puzzle over trauma from that night, waiting patiently. Father received intelligence rebels were there, so we delayed our forces until they moved out.

Oh.

"We had just left the day before. I had an urgent message from another territory, but my first mate insisted we stay." She whispers, her eyes never leaving mine, "we heard about what happened *after* realizing the note was a fraud, and I learned my lesson that day to never doubt him again."

"I didn't mean for any of that to happen, this bond … " I crack, unsure why I feel the need to explain myself to her, or perhaps I need to speak my circumstance aloud to someone who has a conscience. "For so long I've done terrible things, because I didn't want to hurt my family." I whisper, glancing at Orion still sound asleep beside me, "but I left anyway, and I'm still a monster."

She rests her hand palm up on my bedside, inches from my blanket covered legs. I raise a brow and surprise myself by taking it, intrigued by the intense warmth I find there. "What matters now is, what are you going to do about it?" She says simply and squeezes my hand, and suddenly excitement washes over me.

"Tell me more about these terms." I say and gently pull away as not to offend her, then cross my arms. She rises and stretches her arms overhead, then strides to the desk with tired steps. The bedroom, if it could be called that, is adjacent to a small washroom tucked into the wall. Maps and navigational equipment line the entire area, as do bits of lace and leather. I flush once more, realizing Orion and I are sleeping in this Captain's bed, and that she must trust us a little to keep us here instead of tied up to the mast.

Orion stirs and slings a heavy arm around me, I groan and slide out from under him. How he's sleeping so heavily is beyond me, usually he's the first one up. Two unfamiliar sets of clothes are neatly folded on the table beside the chair where 'Captain' was, and a shudder rides through my back. I glance over my shoulder to the female still perusing papers at her desk.

"Don't look unless you want a free show." I mutter and receive a grunt in return, then slip my undershorts off and hurriedly pull on thick dark breeches.

Next is a long sleeved navy tunic with fine white embroidery detailing the cotton fabric. Leathers lined with tawny furs pile on top of my other layers, and I find my weapons in a neat pile on the floor. Dagger hurriedly find homes in leather belts and I sheathe my sword in it's scabbard at my side. Everything fits perfectly, and the quality is above average. Lastly I pull on wool socks and fur lined leather boots, then a giddy feeling fills me. I might see snow.

After dressing I turn and find a very confused Orion sitting up in bed, glancing between the Captain and I. I give him a wide smile and muss back my tangled hair, but he frowns. "Don't tell me you're *already* sleeping with her."

I laugh heartily, the sound echoing through the cabin as my wall between us subconsciously rises, as it always does when *those* memories haunt me. Little does Orion know, 'sleeping' with half of Silverbury wasn't my choice, and he doesn't need to know any different. Surprisingly, the melodic Captain finds humor in his statement as well.

"No worries smart one, I have no taste for males." She admits with confidence, and I blink.

Of course *I* have no problems finding attraction in the same sex, but it's generally not something Fae openly admit, unless they're looking for trouble. I stride to the Captain leaning against her desk and grin, facing a very flushed Orion. He's never had *any* interest in females, or risking his life in figuring out if he does like males.

I probably know him better than he knows himself, in that aspect.

"No faith in me, O? She was merely," I narrow my brows together as I sling an arm around her shoulders, sensing we're going to be fast friends, "what is your name again?"

"Captain." She smirks, shrugging off my arm with casual strength I didn't anticipate.

"*Just* Captain?" Orion asks after finding his glasses resting on a small table beside his side of the bed, squinting at Captain through the cracked lens.

"You know, *I* call you the smart one. Don't make me doubt it." Captain drawls, leaving my side to retrieve a stack of papers from her desk.

"Well, what does that make me?" I pout.

She laughs and mutters something under her breath, then hands me the stack which sobers me immediately. Orion dresses in warm similar clothing to myself while I read through Captain's reports of nearly every disappearance that's occurred in the past decade, and every case is linked to us. Orion comes to my side and I hand him off what I've read thus far, then my heart stops when I'm left holding the report about Vabel.

A once thriving Sylvan fishing village populated with hundreds of Fae and some fifty odd brave humans, reduced to nothing. Next is the official declaration from Silverbury accusing Borealis of declaring war on their border town. Reports detail the human inventions of crossbows at the scene and no human were bodies found, courtesy of me and an unwilling Loyska. She didn't like being made to clean up her mess, especially by the *Prince* who wouldn't give her what she wanted. What everyone wants from me.

"It's done now, Al. Maybe we can help fix the mess **we** *made. Loyska used to be somebody, it isn't her fault we made her into a monster, and she's at peace now."* Orion offers over the bond and I look up to find him trying on a smile. I hadn't realized he could hear me, so I only nod with tight lips and shuffle the papers back together, then set them carefully on her desk. I strengthen my wall once more, suppressing memories of fucking on display for the world to see, like a prized stallion.

"I have two questions." Orion states and Captain whirls around in the plush high backed chair she had settled in during our study. She gestures for him to continue, pale fingers knitted in her lap.

"What do you want us to do, and how is it you can so confidently provide protection? People are going to know who we are, and I'm sure it won't be long before Typhan retaliates." Orion glances at me, then Captain with unfamiliar confidence, he looks so much stronger in this atmosphere. "He's been waiting for this day, I'm sure he's planned for repercussions."

Captain rises and smiles, crossing her arms. "I'm counting on it. I hate to say it, but the bigger the drama, the harder it'll be for the other courts to turn a blind eye any longer."

"So, you *want* Typhan to find us?" Orion asks, fists clenched and glasses sliding down his sharp nose.

"He already knows where we are O, it was too easy for us to leave. No, he wants to play a game with us, using Iverbourne as his board."

50

I say with annoyance, and Orion glares at me. *"I can be the smart one sometimes, too, jackass."*

Captain clears her throat and circles around the desk, then stands between us silently insulting the other. "Indeed he already knows where you are, look at this." She extends a coffee stained parchment to me and I recognize Mother's handwriting at once. A list of names, and nothing else. The name written in haste at the very top is near indiscernible.

Marta.

"Who is that?" Orion asks, peering through his glasses. The healers said our 'circumstances' of birth rendered him almost entirely blind, a soul deep injury that Aether cannot fix. I swallow overwhelming emotions and cross my arms tight.

"*That* is who we are going to see, Marta is the Chieftess of Farhaven. Isn't that a wonderful coincidence? We made a deal last year, a trade route between Hallowed and Borealis, given I could rescue as many humans as possible out of Sylvan." Captain muses, finger tapping on Marta's name.

"So that's why you were in Sylvan, you really were Mother's smuggler?" I demand, slow moving anger flowing through me at our now dead Mother. After all this time, she never stopped fighting, and led me to believe she did. Whether it be from my own resolve breaking or her own, she always planned on dying at Father's hand.

"Yes, for several years now, though that was the first time we met. As you can understand, working around a bond requires exploiting some *major* loopholes. My first mate conducted most of my business and she had a young female conducting hers. We knew this heist would be the last for awhile." Captain explains, removing her hat and stroking the colored feather upon it. Charis, after all this time, she's been helping too?

"What is this list then, why is her name on it if she's not someone to save?" Orion asks, frowning at Captain who is somber. She wrinkles her pointed nose and glances between us, pausing for a subtle moment on my blanched face.

"This is a list of all the underground allies Typhan has made in the last year, though I was not able to receive this information until my visit, nor are their connections to Typhan clear. All we know for now is the friend of our enemy, is our enemy."

"That makes no sense, he is literally known for his throne of *human* bones. He violates them and-" I nearly fall into a rush of traumatic scenarios and Orion rests a hand on my shoulder, calming my heart and pulling me from the anxiety filled abyss. I pass the note back to Captain with a trembling hand and cross my arms, hiding my shakiness.

"I have to agree with my brother, what use would he have for a Human Chieftess? She's not even the Queen of the Court, unless she's supplying slaves from the outer communities without the Queen knowing ..." Orion trails off, rubbing his chin.

Captain shrugs and hands him the note, but he doesn't take it. "It's not me you have to trust, it's your Mother. I, for one, am curious to see what happens when we land, if they are in league together, I bet Marta will be surprised to see us so soon."

"Soon?" Orion asks as I wander through lost cyclical thoughts.

"We're three months early, there were some questionable events that led me to take surprise as a friend, which lended itself handy to you two." I avoid Captain's stare, there's no way she could possibly know I would've ended it all by the time they arrived.

Sorrow fills me suddenly and I lock away the realization that I would've tried again, before Orion can hear it.

Before he can hear the fact that the call of death still hounds my haunted steps, and my bloodstained heart is tired. If I keep thinking about Orion, weariness lifts long enough for me to keep going. A flash of Novak's sapphire eyes send my heart into a wild thunder and I force myself to keep breathing, rubbing my neck with a shaky hand.

Orion nods, studying Captain and oblivious to my self induced plight. "So, what do we do?"

"It so happens I am in need of a Quartermaster and Master of Arms, both positions were occupied by someone who has moved on to new adventures," Captain focuses her softened attention on me, "and admittedly my first mate could use some pointers on directing his Aether, I hear you specialize in Aether combat."

I clasp my hands behind my back, finding resolve and strength somehow. "So you want us to be a part of this protect and rescue crew, to what end, though? You can't be everywhere and protect everyone, all the time."

"I never suggested otherwise, I just help as many as I can and ensure to leave them better protected than when I found them. Besides my first mate and myself, you two are the most powerful here and have a wealth of inside knowledge, something I would consider payment for your stay. No one is capable of saving everyone, not even you, dear Prince."

I bristle and prepare to hurl a retort but Orion beats me to it. "If we only get Captain for a name, then you drop this Prince shit. And let's get another thing straight, if you think we're proud of anything we did, you better let us off this ride now."

I smile and clap a hand on Orion's shoulder. *"You're growing, little brother."*

"Seriously, three minutes Al."

"We have a deal then." She decides with satisfaction and paces away to a wide door at the opposite end of the room, pausing with her hand on the knob. "Come out when you're ready and we'll show you to your quarters, then we'll be landing in a few hours and I expect you both ready to help."

"Help?" I ask, curious what she would need us to do in Human lands other than act as bait. She smiles, then opens the door which reveals boisterous music and chatter on the ship beyond. Captain leaves us, gently shutting the door which silences the music at once. Orion pushes up his glasses and sighs, his once hopeful face now somber.

"I can hear Mother, still." He admits at once, hands fidgeting. I rest one hand on his shoulder and cup his wet cheek with my other.

"Me too. Let's make her proud, ok?" I whisper and he nods, "You and me, that's how we live."

"And never falter." He replies with tears trailing into my palm. I fold him into a tight hug and we remain alone for a while before facing our new world.

II

Beyond the Wall

How much worse can it get?

I am not at all prepared for the full beauty of Captain's airship, and the fact only she seems to be powering the beast is nerve wracking. Usually air crews use their collective Aether to power the heavy engines, but every gawking crew mate staring at us thus far lacks a glow to their various eye colors. Orion and I stand in the middle of organized chaos on the main deck, he and I both marveling at the galleon and struck stupid.

First to demand my attention are the grand golden sails. The main mast's trapezoidal sail dominates the others in size and holds a faerie skull and crossbones, it's taut wide fabric catching the last dwindling sun rays filled with dusk. A smaller triad of triangular gaff sails stretch from the prow rigging at the front of the ship and meet the square sails of the foremast fluttering over Orion and I's head.

A matching triad of triangular sails attach to the main mast at the center of the ship and catch wind over Captain's head at the stern, where she watches the smaller than average air ship crew begin to release knots and take in sails. I marvel at just how much golden fabric fills the ship from stern to prow, contrasting most airships which use one or two sails at most. Orion is studying every aspect of the ship, memorizing the process at once, a feat I'm quite often jealous of. Nightfall creeps from the east, I can't believe we slept for an entire day. High and Lesser Fae alike tend to the rigging as gentle flames lick Captain's shoulders at the helm, and she winks when I catch her burning crimson eyes. I don't know why I expected the crew to be composed solely of Fire Fae, but Air and Earth Fae alike glare at us, and even a pair of horned Lesser Fae stare as they wander past.

Orion tugs on my sleeve and I follow his gaze to a raised level over the prow, what appears to be a dining area filled with humans. I recognize a few of them as servants from the castle, and they certainly recognize us. I avert my eyes and my neck warms, air caught in my broad chest. I wonder where the children are, I haven't seen them or the group of healers Captain said tended to our wounds. I imagine fragile cargo is quite common and Captain has them tucked away somewhere quiet, she seems to have a kind heart in that way.

"Must be they're going home." Orion whispers and I nod. His glacial worry leaks over the bond and I shudder. *"I really don't want to go there, how influential do you think she is? You've killed a lot of-"*

"Thanks for reminding me, I almost forgot." I snap and walk away from his side. A gentle breeze ruffles my inky hair and I sigh, then shove my hands in my pockets whilst retreating to the railing. I peer over the edge into the sea of thin purple and pink clouds we fly through, the distant sun nearly captured by the horizon. A smile escapes me as I watch a large flock of sea birds travel alongside the ship, but a pang of loneliness strikes my heart.

"Heard I get to deal with you a lot more from now on, can't say I'm too thrilled."

I startle and glance down at the *Zemer* beside me, curls catching wind and eyes kindled with that furious blue fire. I chuckle and cross my arms to match his stiff stance, casually looking around to find Orion talking with Captain at the helm. He must've gotten the hint I don't want to talk.

"Oh come now, I'm not all bad. Here, let's start over." I thrum my fist to my chest and bow farther than I ever have to Typhan, then rise with a smile. "Alvis."

He rolls his eyes, playful smile revealing deep set dimples. His hands drop to his sides and after another moment of contemplation, he returns the show of respect. "Novak, first mate to our dear Captain." Novak announces proudly, gesturing to the busy galleon.

"*Oh, so you're* the first mate I'm supposed to be training? This shall be fun." I taunt and he groans, shaking hair away from his eyes.

"I don't need *training* because Captain can't handle my skills." He obnoxiously shouts, giving Captain a wink when she glares down at him from the helm.

I take a casual step closer, towering over him. His right ear twitches and a once steady pulse quickens in his neck, smile widening with mischief. Despite the chill he's only wearing a plain grey sweater and loose chestnut trousers that tuck into his knee high leather boots.

"What's the matter, afraid I might be able to kick your ass when I'm sober?" I taunt playfully and he grins, straightening. He's a few inches shorter than I am, but his cocky presence makes up for it.

"Highly doubt it." Novak stops himself before he can say Prince and studies my face with sudden intensity. Flashing violet reflects in his wide eyes as my magic sparks. I cannot look away even if I wanted to, and I feel like this is a test of some sort. For a split second we are captivated and pressed against the other, then Novak dives for my waist.

I dance out of the way, sticking a boot out to trip the musician. He tumbles down and hooks my ankle with his, taking me down with him. Hearty laughter erupts around us as our good natured scuffle commences. Novak's beaming smile never leaves, the swift Fae dodging every swipe and side stepping every approach I take.

Fighting has always reminded me of dancing. Swordplay reminds me of a classical harmony in a ballroom, precise movements and steps. Hand to hand combat reminds me of nights filled with music like Novak's, when the tune is unpredictable and keeps you on your toes. I finally connect with his jaw and he staggers backwards with a cracked grin, I didn't intend for so much force but he doesn't seem to mind.

"You're a slippery little thing, I'll give you that." I roll my neck and wipe sweat from my brow, he throws his head back and howls with joy. Sweat trails down his neck, dampening his collar, and I focus on his suddenly indecisive footwork instead of how good it would feel to trace those glistening beads down his chest.

"Oh, it's been awhile since I've had a good scrap, can't say you're too bad yourself." Novak taunts, simmering eyes sparking my soul to life in front of the whole crew. Heat spreads from my core throughout my body, as he approaches and I suddenly find myself paralyzed. As he feigns a hit to my face, a solid fist connects with my gut.

"Are you going to make yourself useful or what?" Captain hollers to the whooping crew. Orion is hunched over and studying something behind her, though I can feel his secondhand embarrassment from here. The crew pats their first mate on the back before dispersing, giving me sidelong glances. Though it was a draw, it seems he was determined their victor.

"Yes, *Ma*." Novak teases Captain, wiping blood from his chin. He gestures for me to follow him to the crew's quarters below. I catch a glimpse of Orion's ingenuity striking fire through the bond as whatever he's studying lights his soul, but his engineering brain screeches to a halt as he catches my own emotions.

Orion straightens on the deck above as if struck by lightning and he groans internally. *"Ohh boy."*

"Shut up, it's nothing." I feebly explain. Orion's echoing laughter is plain through our connection and I fight the urge to curse him out.

60

"Problem?" Novak asks, waiting at the top of the ladder leading below deck with a raised brow. I shake my head, confused as to why he would ask. "Your face was funny, then again, you always look funny, so." He shrugs before climbing down the ladder.

"Take it you've never met a twin before?" I ask while following him down, surprise hitting me when I find how large the lower deck is. Hammocks line the space, suspended between columns, and a small kitchen is centered in the midst of it. Colorful tapestry doors line the outer space and two wooden doors rest on a far end. Soft childish laughter flows from a red tapestry to my right and I smile.

"Perhaps, why?" Novak throws over his shoulder, leaving me behind as he paces to the kitchen area composed of cupboards, counter islands and stools. I follow him over and bite my cheek, unsure why I'm telling him this.

"Well, they're your other half, of your soul that is. You're born with them, instead of having to find them." I mutter and he pauses in the midst of opening cupboards and showing off their fully stocked goods, contemplating me with a softened expression.

"I didn't know that. I thought your fated was supposed to be your partner, the person you love." Novak says thoughtfully, now light blue eyes glazed over. I shrug, fighting the rising hunger inside me while exotic smells flow into my nostrils. There's enough food here to feed the entire Outer Rim.

"I do love my brother, obviously not in the way *you're* thinking, but I don't think your fated has anything to do with love, it's just the rest of your soul."

I'm not entirely sure how we got on this subject of love, but I pace around the square of cupboards and join him in the center. I wipe blood from his cheek with my sleeve and he flinches, so I take a casual step back.

"My point is, we can talk, using our bond. I suppose that's why my face was 'funny' as you called it, he was picking on me." I grin, but his handsome face is now pulled tight. The sparring Fae who smiled at me above is gone now, and an urge to smooth the wrinkles from his brow passes me.

"My friend, the one in that place," Novak wavers and clears his throat, then speaks flatly. "He was a twin, his brother was my friend. I imagine it works the same for humans as it does Fae, the bond, that is."

How did such an innocuous conversation suddenly turn so dark? I clench my jaw and fists as he inhales deeply, eyes wandering the quarters as my shoulders fall.

"Probably good thing they're both dead, otherwise I'd imagine it hurt like hell to live without your other half." Glacial daggers spike his voice and I shove my hands in my pants pockets.

"Yes, I imagine so." I whisper, then summon courage and search his eyes. I expect fury, but light blue flames have softened to a deep luminescent ocean. The magic emanating from them is so bright, he must be powering the ship right now. Novak runs a hand through his hair and sighs, so I take my chance. I reach to rest a hand on his shoulder but think better of it, shoving it back into my pocket.

"I know the words I'm sorry and I had no choice are inconsequential, but I have agreed to work with Captain. Not because I want protection, but because I want to make it right. Or try, even if it takes a lifetime. I don't expect your forgiveness, and if you are uncomfortable with my being here, we shall leave."

Novak nods, and I expect a grand monologue or at least a smart ass comment, but instead he gestures to two purple fabric doors off to the side before slipping away. "Those are set up for you two, the hammocks are for travelers. If you'll excuse me." Before I can say anything he struts away and slips behind a blue tapestry on the opposite side of the quarters.

Well, it's a start.

* * *

Night sweeps over the ship and the glowing city of Farhaven waits below Captain's hovering galleon. Everyone from the crew to the small group of humans is surrounding the towering center mast and facing the helm where Captain and Novak are standing, faces serious. Behind them are the four children and three female Water Fae, they must be the healers. Captain's glowing red eyes intensify when she speaks and I stiffen beside Orion, both of us hiding near foremast, away from the center of the ship.

"You are officially home my friends, though I've enjoyed your company, I hope I *never* see you again." Captain proclaims, tossing her hat high into the air and catching it with ease. Cheers erupt along Fae and Humans alike and my charcoal ears fold down, heart beating with warmth and guilt equally. Novak watches Captain with pride and a soft smile, and I wonder how many times she's said that.

The entire crew is delighted with the successful mission, she's employed so many different misfits it's hard to keep them all straight. The Air and Water Fae at the helm smile, but their joy isn't as intense as the humans around me. Of course, they still have another journey after this before they can go home. Fae and Humans have only just begun interacting with each other since the war, Borealis isn't a safe place for them to live. Really, no where is safe for the less fortunate, because of people like me.

The eldest child connects eyes with me and interrupts my spiral of thoughts, her skin nearly revived and rosy shoulder length hair glowing under the numerous warm globe lanterns lighting the ship. She smiles, and suddenly I feel much better.

"Master of arms, eh?" Orion elbows me and I startle, flashing lilac lighting up his delighted face. His inky coils match my own perfectly, but his shine much brighter under the lanterns than mine do, and they reach down to his hips when it's loose. I don't think it's been tied up at all since we've left, due to freedom or lack of lab work I'm not sure.

"Fancy for muscle I bet, Quartermaster sounds better. I saw you gawking at something up there, how's her tech?" I gesture to the helm and watch chaos unfold around us at the foremast, studying the landing process. Novak suggested we watch this go around, but insisted we wouldn't get off easily next time.

"Al, you wouldn't *believe* the size of the engines, the scopes she's got and-" He immediately launches into a full fledged course on her navigational systems and custom Aether efficient mechanics, but I stop listening about halfway through. Novak shouts orders to the crew as he paces back and forth across the ship, adding playful smiles and jokes to soften his authority. There are so many sides to him, and I care for them all.

A roguish troublemaker, authoritative figure, loyal first mate and friend to his Captain. A *Zemer* who can enchant crowds and a Water Fae who disdains our kind just as much as I do, with Aether unlike any I've ever seen. I wonder if he's always fought evil, and intuition tells me the answer is yes.

An annoyed sigh rolls from beside me and my cheeks flush.

"Sorry, it all sounds great, O. Might not be so bad being pirates after all." I nervously smile and rub my neck. Orion chuckles and rakes a slender vined hand through his curls, the only indication he heard my inner monologue. My tattoos and his have nearly healed now, though phantom pain is still very much apparent for him and I both, searing flames constantly crawling under our skin.

Novak calls us over and teaches us the basics of the rigging whilst the crew finishes the landing process, which he explains occurs only *after* the Aether engines turn down. Unless you want the ship to flip over, apparently. First he corrects me on my wordage, the ship is specifically a brig, defined by the fact it has two masts and numerous stay sails between them, the triangular sails. If I wasn't already lost, the various halyard and sheet rigging tangles up my mind further, so many parts have interchangeable names that makes my eyes water.

Novak is straightforward and surprisingly humorless as he gives us both a crash course. Orion already knows more than I do, of course, and I find myself struggling to keep up with the first mate hurriedly tracing back and forth across the ship. Even at night his honeyed hair seems to glimmer, and even more hidden freckles glow under the fresh slivers of gold and silver moonlight.

*"**Ugh**, are you going to just gawk at him or do something about it?"* Orion snarks and I groan inwardly whilst staying put with him beside the ornate railing while Novak leaves us temporarily to find someone named Hugo. I cross my arms and face the approaching airport beneath us, and Orion turns his back to the ship as well.

*"I'm not **gawking**, I'm just, thankful is all."* For such a nice view, that is. Fuck, I seriously do need to get myself together.

"Right ..." Orion's lecture is interrupted as a solid shove to my side nearly takes me off my feet and I involuntarily snarl. My reflexes send me towering over an elder man in a second. My hackles lower slightly at the sight of the gangly human, though his hate filled eyes keep me on guard. Orion is vigilant at my side and his sudden fury gives me a headache. Skin tags pull along the man's frown and he rubs his dark chin, making a show of the fact he only has two fingers.

"Apologies, thought I saw a *benzonna* there." He spits on my dark leather boots and raises a bushy peppered brow, the small group of middle aged humans around him chuckling. I bristle at his insult but reign in my rising Aether, palms open and deep breaths forcing themselves through me. *We need them to see you on our side.*

"Ah, must've been your attitude instead." I pat the human on his shoulder and smile wide, then Orion and I leave the humans. We find refuge on the helm beside Captain, having lost Novak. The children and healers are gone and once we're by her side I spy him on the main deck below. His light brows narrow upon seeing us on the helm, but as the ground approaches he turns his attention elsewhere.

"Problem?" Captain asks with a raised angled brow, attention otherwise focused on the steering wheel and her crew below.

"Nay." I say curtly and she nods, then launches into a discussion with Orion over his views on alternative methods to Aether fuel. I cross my arms and study the mountainous terrain around us, and a small part of me is sad there's no snow waiting for us. Borealis lands are entirely different from the wheat lands of Sylvan, though the only time I've left Silverybury's walls to explore was to abduct Fae in the night, and that was only in nearby Terra and Hallowed outlands.

Borealis is full of valleys and mountains cutting through the rocky alpine land, deep green coniferous trees dot the grey landscape and wind beaten brush is scattered along the craggy cliff sides. I've heard the capitol has a grand castle made of ice, but the town we finally touch down in reminds me of a toned down version of Cervalis. Towering brick buildings and trees surround the simple airport, waiting to embrace the giant ship. Farhaven is nestled in the midst of a deep valley, thick with trees and epic unmovable stones left over from ancient glaciers.

A solid thud echoes through the ship as it docks on freshly built scaffolding, a cradle for the ship to rest in. All of the docking ports are brand new, but we are the only ship here. The ramp unfolds and lets loose the crew, joyous humans and other travelers.

"Was this port crafted before or after you visited?" I ask, drawing Captain's attention.

"We couldn't land last time, the scaffolding was in poor condition, and unless anything's changed, we're the only ship allowed landing permits." She replies with a sly smile. "Why?"

"If you're not meant to be here for another three months after the ground warms, why would they build this in the middle of winter? They'll have to start over again once the soil shifts, if their trade is only from the High Court as you say and not overseas, seems odd to me is all."

"Interesting." Orion pushes up his glasses, glancing between Captain and I.

"They could've built it before the frost." Captain counters, though her eyes are lit with delight.

"Nay, the altitude is higher here, from what I've heard winter hits two months earlier and leaves two months earlier here as well. Another couple of months it'll be spring here, plenty of time to build one docking station for their only incoming ship."

"And there's a lot more than one station." Orion affirms. "Appears it's the semi circle design, and there's space for 12 ships if my sight isn't failing me."

"It isn't, there's twelve." Novak says as he leaps onto the helm from the ladder. My heart beats in tune with every step he takes closer to me. He joins our tight discussion, shaking wild hair from his eyes. "Everyone's out. Why does the design matter?"

"Semi circles are reserved for well to do trading centers, though it's on a cliff, Cervalis' is fashioned the same way, and I've heard the port outside Terra is as well. Silverbury's airport was too small to form the design, we only had two docking stations." I explain to Novak plainly, hoping it doesn't come off as condescending, though I'm surprised he doesn't know. All three of my companions stare at me in anticipation.

"When the Ancients first taught Fae how to wield their gift of technology and airships, the very first airport they built in Iverbourne was a gorgeous semi circle port stretching miles wide, hosting a trading center for the entire world, before Iverbourne was severed from it's neighbors. Silverbury is built on the remains of the once grand city gifted to us. From the bits of knowledge I stole from the restricted section of the castle library, the crescent was an important shape for the Ancients, but I never learned why."

Orion snickers and I glare at him. "What?"

"I never knew you snuck into the library, why didn't you take me with you?"

"Because I didn't want to put you in anymore danger than you already were." My cheeks flush, I didn't mean to speak that aloud, let alone so bluntly.

His once playful face falters, but Captain saves us. "We'll stay here for two nights." Captain removes her hat and combs through her hair, then returns it upon her crown.

"And then?" Orion asks matter of factually, pushing up his glasses. Novak bounces on his heels and glances between Captain and I, grinning. She rolls her eyes and throws her hands up in his direction, feigning annoyance.

"We'll be going to *Headquarters.*" Novak says mysteriously, hands expressively stretching out the word. Captain laughs, leaning on the steering wheel.

Exhaustion takes over her features and I wonder how she powers this thing day after day, even with Novak's help. I chuckle as does Orion, but then we all sober after a moment. Captain focuses on Novak and a serious mask falls back over his face, hands planted on his hips. He's still only wearing a sweater, despite the gusts of icy wind blowing through my cloak and numerous layers.

"Eyes and ears open, that is all." Captain's crimson eyes connect with mine and don't leave until I nod, and she repeats with Orion, then Novak.

"Sure thing Cap, though it amazes me you can accomplish such legendary deals even in your sleep." Novak winks, smiling as he bounds for the ladder. Where does he get his energy?

"Pain in the ass." Captain mutters, waving him off as she stands and stretches her arms overhead. Novak climbs down the ladder without another word, then dives to the crew's quarters below.

"You won't be going?" Orion asks from behind me as I follow the first mate. She contemplates him for a moment, pausing my step.

"No, the legend of Captain tells itself much better when people don't see the *actual* Captain. Novak takes care of business, and I the ship. It's the way it's always been. Go with him, tell the world you're on my ship." Orion and I glance at each other, and she doesn't miss it. "You'll be fine, and we need people to see you on our side."

Captain leaves the helm for the main deck, cutting in front of Orion and I. We follow behind in contemplative silence. I cannot help but grasp her arm before she retreats into her cabin below the helm. Her eyes alight and she scowls, causing my hand to drop. I open my lips but don't know what to say, so she marches into her quarters and slams the door in my face.

"You'll be fine, *trust* me." Novak calls and I glare over my shoulder at the handsome Fae waiting at the top of the ramp, laden with a pack and lute.

Orion shrugs and trails after the *Zemer.* "How much worse can it get?"

Zemer.

Outside of the semi circle airport is an inclined dirt road, worn down by frozen wagon tracks in the mud. I study the tracks, finding multiple sets going back and forth from the airport. We aren't planning on unloading until the morning, which means in the past few days someone has utilized the airport.

At the end of that winding road is a human village, full of life and ornately built longhouses painted in whites and blues shadowed by near midnight darkness. I've never seen Humans of so many ages, so many varying degrees of wrinkles and wear. Normally Sylvan's mercenaries take only the young from any race, and usually only female humans. Aging has always fascinated me. Fae can live for an eternity if they want to, but we always tend to kill each other before that happens.

Children bounce through the stretching longhouse we are settled in and a grand fire pit lines the center space. A four foot tall wall of large stones cradle layers of embers and coals, providing warmth to every inch of the communal hall. The vertical wooden planks of the walls curve inwards, reminding me of the rounded hull of a ship. Humans of fair complexion share painted white runes on their faces, and plaits of gold are also common among all the men and women. Steel grey and tinted blue eyes stare from every direction, lacking Aether when their passion or anger flares.

No one gives Orion and I a second glance here. The humans we arrived with had dispersed to their respective long lost homes immediately, no longer concerned with us. The Chieftess requested a meeting with us and her inner council at once, which seems to be half the tribe to me. Two soldiers stopped us at the door to the tavern across town, just as we anticipated they would. Novak sits cross legged on the dirt floor packed with ashes at one end of the coals, and the young Chieftess rests at the other.

Marta of Farhaven.

Orion and I are situated on either side of Novak, the rest of his crew is happily visiting old friends and an open bar supplied with mead behind Orion. A thriving kitchen is behind me, and it unnerves my spirit to not have every person in the longhouse in my viewpoint. Novak keeps the fair woman with white finger marks of paint down both sides of her round face in a hard stare, his calm face unchanging as they have an entire silent exchange.

I can't help but note Marta is Typhan's typical type, albeit a bit muscular perhaps.

"Do you think they're talking like we do?" Orion ponders, fidgeting across the crackling fire from me. Elders wrung with labor and battle scars rest in quiet patience around the handsome mousy haired Chieftess and after ten minutes of the two staring at the other in silence, they begin laughing.

"Nay, I believe it was just a very long staring contest. Perhaps a custom of theirs."

"*Ai*, if I lost twice in a row I know I'd *never* live it down." Novak chuckles, hands folded in his lap.

"Oy Zemer, I must admit I did not expect to see you so quickly, or to show up unannounced in the night. Not that I'm complaining, it's just that Sylvan is known for its impenetrable defenses, and I've missed you terribly, you know." She muses, her attention set on Novak as she flutters her long blonde lashes. Red flag number one.

Although she is quite petite, bone and bead necklaces similar to Typhan's rest atop grey wolf furs wrapped tight around her shoulders. The sparking fire illuminates a road map of scars upon her expressive hands, lending further to the wolf in a sheep's clothing presence I sense from her. I wonder what kind of Fae she'd be if she had Aether, the gleam in her calculating eyes makes me think Water.

"*Ai,* we had a late night and I couldn't wait on the ship, nor could I bring myself to wake you at this hour. Captain hoped to bring home more of your comrades, but as you can understand, plans go awry. They plan on returning in the spring to liberate more." Novak speaks with a humble confidence I have not heard before, and it has my dick twitching. Orion groans over the bond and I resolve to put up another small wall between us regarding *certain* feelings. Never again will we be *fully* cut off from each other, though.

"Indeed, and I will hold you to that promise. I shall never doubt you or your Captain again, though I am delighted to meet them." Her full smile tightens and Novak stiffens, but his smile doesn't falter through the elated whispers floating around.

Did you hear that? They're going back.

The Captain is going to save more of us.

Luck is bound to run out.

Fae are only in it for themselves, they'll betray us.

Just you wait.

"You know how it works, my dear *nagid.*" Honey drips from his words and the Chieftess blushes. Though I don't know the word, I'm sure it's a compliment. Vanity is plain in her rosy cheeks, the need to be desired after is something Humans and Fae share.

"Very well." She turns her attention to Orion and receives his show of respect, then her eyes dilate wide as she focus on me. I press a fist to my chest, ears warming as I bow my head under her heated stare. An elongated wooden smoking device passes to me after and I give the squat elder woman who gave it to me a soft smile, which she warmly returns. I scrutinize the citrusy herb stuffed into the ornate peace pipe, then light it with a match and inhale deep.

"Perhaps you can tell me who these strapping Fae are?" I almost choke on the earthy smoke entering my lungs whilst passing the pipe to a smirking Novak. I've smoked herbs before, but the quality here is so striking it literally takes my breath away. The musician inhales deeply and gestures to me first, then my brother.

"Oh yes, we have new friends. I'm sure you've heard of the *Te'Omin.*" The entire longhouse stops moving, and every head snaps to us. I force myself to remain unfazed, and Orion just casually puffs on the pipe then passes it along, though I can feel his panic. The elders surrounding the Chieftess murmur, and she waves them off with a sly grin.

"As a gift? You're too kind." Marta's silver eyes catch on me and she licks her lips, slick panic rolls through my body as her throat bobs. Unwanted memories of Typhan 'lending' me like a prized stud to hungry noble females and males alike churns my stomach. Orion's fists tighten immediately, his face and hands blanch so immensely that Novak's attention turns to him. Novak's windswept hair lit up by firelight breaks me from my nightmare and I realize what happened.

For the first time, I couldn't bury the trauma far enough so Orion couldn't see.

Fuck.

"*Nay,*" Novak affirms with a hard glare, "they are part of my crew, and will answer any questions you have."

"*Al, I didn't even-*"

"*It's nothing, O. I don't want to talk about it.*" I snap down the bond between us, focusing on the fire as Orion continues to stare at me with pity, which burns into my soul. Silence crawls inside my head and out for a moment, then I focus strongly on the Chieftess with my usual charm.

"What he says is true, I am Alvis," I press a hand to my chest, then gesture to Orion, "and this is my brother Orion. Though it shall take more than one lifetime to provide recompense, we are both prepared to offer our services."

The flash of hunger in the Chieftess' strong eyes makes me wish I used different wording, and Novak shifts uncomfortably beside me. I don't have anything against humans, but I recognize the insatiable hunger in her that most who seek power hold. They feel entitled to anything, even people. Red flag number too many.

"*Indeed*, more than a lifetime. I am Marta, Chieftess of Farhaven. Friends of the *Zemer* and Captain are friends of ours, are they not?"

Cheers erupt through the longhouse, every face turned up in delight. Several disgruntled humans remain on the sidelines, but a general air of ease falls over the night. Chants of *Zemer* fill the air and Novak raises his hands, shaking his head. "*Ai,* already?" He groans, though he retrieves the lute strapped to his back, settling it into his lap with a soft smile. We need something to break the tension.

A small tawny skinned child tugs on Orion's sleeve and reaches for his glasses, my brother obliges and watches with a smile as the young thing looks through them and goes cross eyed. I laugh and hold my stomach, several others joining in with hearty laughter and local tales quickly follow. Novak strums a soft tune on the multitude of strings, much gentler than the first time I heard him play. I find myself staring at the instrument, quite a simple and beaten up thing for a *Zemer* who doesn't even take tips. His face is different when he plays, though he smiles and puts on a good show, peace radiates from his eyes so intensely I can feel it from here.

A gentle hand rests on my shoulder, disrupting my moment. It takes everything inside me not to jolt as I look up to find Marta standing over me, the jaws of both wolves composing her furs are eye level with my face. A light hand traces up my frozen neck and pets the fluff on my folded ear like a dog. A shiver runs down my paralyzed spine and Marta laughs, her body filled with the haunting sound. "I would like your company Prince, *your* services should provide recompense enough."

"*Ai*, my friends stay put with me," Novak's primal tone reverberates through my chest, his calm command lifts Marta's hand from my skin, "Captain's orders." He doesn't miss a beat as he starts a new tune, keeping her in his hardened gaze until she moves. Marta's hazel brows draw together but she smiles, dipping her chin. I choke on nightmares, air catching in my lungs until she steps back reluctantly. Orion stares at her and I internally ask him to stop.

"Of course." She says, glaring at me over her shoulder before resuming her post at the head of the hearth.

The rest of the evening commences without a hitch, Novak cementing a permanent trade deal between Borealis and Hallowed Court, using Farhaven as a trade center. How Captain came to work for Hallowed Court is another question I haven't had answered yet, or how a Fire Fae made friends with humans in the first place. The Chieftess doesn't seem like someone Captain would do business with, Marta reminds me so much of my father it hurts.

I find myself in Marta's attention several more times but the rest of the humans keep me busy enough to politely ignore her, and Novak's exuberant presence is oddly comforting. Despite his scrawny appearance, the Fae holds much more strength than meets the eye, and his ballads of adventures with Captain are never ending. I wonder if they've always been together, as I haven't heard any tales otherwise.

When I catch Orion laughing heavily, body relaxed from smoke and good company, some of the guilt from letting my guard down washes away. Novak's own dimple filled smile has me staring at the handsome male for a moment too long, but he doesn't look away. My heart trips over itself and sudden courage has me opening my lips to say something terribly stupid. Of course, the moment is broken by shouts emerging from outside the longhouse.

Novak, Orion and I jump up at the same time, but Marta and her warriors are already out the door. Snow filled wind nips my face and overlapping screams intertwine with fury. Waiting outside the longhouse is a steaming mound of bloated bodies, the entire village out in the chill and watching with devastation. Orion and I spot her at the same time and sprint to the pile of flesh infused with putrid water, though I stop short as my brother drops to his knees in the fresh dusting of snow. "Orion, don't."

He ignores me and picks up our mother's decapitated head with shaking hands, then howls with such fury the ground shakes beneath us. I bite my cheek until copper immensely fills my mouth. Mother's face is at peace, like it was in the tunnel, if you look beneath the gallons of unnatural water puffing up her skin. Novak rushes to my side and rests a warm hand on my shoulder and I startle, then look down to his somber face upturned to mine.

"Sylvan opened an Aether hole and dumped this here, it looks like everyone we couldn't save." He swallows and focuses on where my gaze is directed, at Orion setting Mother's head precariously on the ground. "How do they even have that much Aether?" Novak whispers, and I stare at him for a moment. All traces of the confident male I've come to know in this short time are gone, replaced by a nervous boy. He doesn't look away, and I finally do after a tense moment.

"It's complicated."

Orion stands, fists shaking and Aether rolling over his body in a luminescent cloud of deep burgundy. I haven't seen him like this in years, and Novak's wide eyes alert me to the fact I'm glowing as well. Blame, hateful words and disgust are directed at Orion and I from the crowd around us. He and I lock eyes, so much pain flowing through us both It's unbearable. Wordlessly, without any idea if it'll work, we both raise our hands towards the pile of dead. Oblivious to the searing heat waiting inside their drowned bodies, and oblivious to the bone chilling cold around us.

Every moment of fear and pain these beings experienced crash over Orion and I like a tidal wave, but we hold steady. Neon purple light spreads through the entire town center we are gathered in, our glowing magic splits the ground and leaves designs of waves and tendrils of vines deep in the frozen dirt around the bodies.

Gasps steal compressed air and shouts of 'what are you doing' meet my ears, but I push it all away. In times like these, Orion and I are truly one. I forget my body, place in space and time, and become one with the Aether, and my other half. Tortured bodies and spirits transform into crystallized translucent fragments of life, and the burning trapped souls release into the atmosphere. Streaks of color shoot into the sky and create a rainbow meteor shower among the stars.

The crystallized bits of broken vessels once inhabited by liberated souls rearrange to form a grand obelisk, over a hundred feet high. When I return to my body and leave the Aether, I am face to face with a tower of living ocean. Everyone steps forward in complete silence and presses a hand to the solid translucent obelisk filled with sea tides, leaving their respects before giving the next in line a turn.

Orion and I lean on the other and shake violently in place as the shimmering neon designs around the obelisk fade, and our Aether depletes to nothing. Novak reaches for me as I fall, trembling hands hold me and Orion both. "What did you two just do?" He whispers. I focus on Novak's flaming blue through my blurred vision, though it's no use.

"No idea." I mumble, then topple over with Orion into darkness.

Mother waits for me in her favorite chair nestled by the fireplace in the grand library, a place I am never allowed to enter unless she's there. I climb into her lap with the body of a young boy and cuddle under her soft arm. "Maman, I missed you." Pure lavender meets my nose and I sigh, peeking down at Orion sleeping in a nest of blankets at her feet.

"Oh and I you darling, but you two must walk with the poet now." She props me up in her lap and taps my nose, then lays tickling kisses all over my slim cheeks. Her bouncing charcoal coils smell like the oil from the trees near the lake, the oil Orion and I picked out for her the year before.

"What is a poet?" I ask through laughter, flashing violet eyes reflected in her own purple irises. She taps her round chin thoughtfully and then raises a finger, struck by a great idea.

"A poet is one who can weave stories of the bravest and smallest, those oft forgotten by history. They do it with such wonder it's as if you're there, fighting side by side against evil."

I scrunch my nose and tilt my head, that makes no sense. "But, if they are the bravest and have tales sung about them, why are the heroes forgotten?" Her always present smile fades and she kisses my wrinkled forehead.

"Evil always finds a way to silence those who fight hardest, my child."

* * *

"I'm telling you, something's not right what that wacko." Novak mutters, incessantly whispering none too quietly to someone. I keep my eyes closed and release a deep sigh, not sure whether to be thankful or exhausted by the fact I'm still alive.

"I never said I disagreed kid, but I have to ask, why do you care so much? You didn't even want him here in the first place." Captain replies, her whisper so full of sass I can picture her brow raising. A heavy moment of pause fills the room and I can't decide what to hope he'll say. I find him to be extraordinary, but I'm also the monster he's hunted for who knows how long.

"I don't, I just think she should've left him alone. Not fit behavior for a Chieftess." A chair creaks beside me with a heavy huff. "She was a thirsty thing before, but something's off about her. Your gut was right, as usual."

"Point made, kid." Captain utters, amusement lighting her voice. Footsteps, only one set, trail away, and silence remains. Soft worry fills my veins when I realize Captain will probably ask me to get close to her.

I've played this game many times before, but every time it's been an order. Sometimes I wonder if Typhan only did it to flex the bond between us, another thing he can force me to do to keep me in check. In my early years I rebelled quite a bit, though Orion resigned to his fate the first day of the bond. The day Typhan caught Charis and I feeding 'property' earned me a special kind of hell, and the thought of being *forced* to lay with anyone ever again sends a rippling shudder through me.

I roll over in bed and stretch, throwing blankets and dark thoughts away. I rest my hands behind my head, finding Novak sitting beside me with eyes wider than the moons. "Morning." I state gruffly, brow raised. I'm still dressed in most of my heavy layers, sans the leathers.

"Sheesh, still alive, thought I was off the hook there for a minute." Novak says, rubbing his neck and smiling nervously. I chuckle and my muscles flex, the bard's eyes flashing with notice as the fabric around my arms tightens.

"Just used a bit too much Aether was all, though I didn't think you'd be one to worry about me." Novak's cheeks flush red and he rises from his chair, standing over me with crossed arms.

"I'm not."

I raise a brow before slowly rising from the bed that must be mine, then stand over him with inches and dizziness between us. "Alright, what're you doing here then?" I whisper, hands trained to my sides instead of where I want them to be. Every part of his perfect soul. Novak's arms loosen and he runs a hand through his crazy hair and sighs. Excitement thrums through me in anticipation of an impossible thing and I focus my breathing, but his wall goes back up.

"Just keeping an eye on you *Te'omin* is all, Captain's orders. *You've* been out for almost a whole day, though I think the smart one has been up for a couple hours now going through Cap's library." Novak quips, usual sarcasm returned. I hide my disappointment and rummage through the modest bedroom for my gear, finding it in a simple walnut dresser at the end of the bed. "We leave tomorrow."

"Great. What does that mean anyway, *Te'omin?*" I mutter in annoyance.

"What, with all your fancy education you didn't learn the Old Language?"

"No, I didn't. Wasn't important enough." I say flatly upon facing him, having no wit. "I only picked up bits and pieces from the slaves."

Novak shoves his hands in his pockets and keeps his curious flashing eyes on me. "*Te'omin* means two bodies, one soul, twins essentially. Though you two are the only famous pair around, so ..." Novak shrugs, his nonchalance transforming into glacial coldness. I grind my teeth and his lips part but I ignore him, strapping on my baldric. I inspect my sword before sheathing it, the familiar sound one I hate to hear. I had no idea how many people know what Orion and I did, and the implications of just how *many* lives we destroyed hits me.

Novak waits with crossed arms in silence, and I respond with a similar stand off attitude. Yes, it's better this way. Too much bad blood, and I'm quite sure he doesn't like males anyway, especially me. Even if he does, I can't drag him into my darkness. Not him, he already matters too much.

"Alright *Zemer*, what's today's plan?"

Hands off.

◆

"You know, when I took the job, I didn't realize there'd be so much mud." I sling muck off my hands and Orion shoves me along the well trodden road on our way back to the ship. The late afternoon sun has warmed the road, twisting ice with slick mud and making unloading supplies difficult. Full laughter throws Novak's head back, the Fae side-stepping the mud hole Orion just shoved me into. "Why thank you, brother."

I rise from the puddle with a wild grin and a yelping Orion uses Novak as a shield. He is a moment too late, a soft orb of lilac Aether and mud twists together and slings across both of their surprised faces. Battle commences and the crew continues past us, leading another caravan of fully loaded wagons from the ship with rolling eyes under the cloudless sky.

I call a truce but Orion dives on me, ruffling my filthy hair whilst he has me pinned on the ground. Echoing laughter fills the valley and I embrace my brother, pulling him down into the mud beside me. Novak is standing beside us with a wild grin, only his sapphire eyes visible under all the mud and matted hair.

For the first time, if only for a moment, I have known true happiness.

Orion and I are still drained from last night, but flames shine in Novak's eyes and within seconds all water and mud is pulled from the three of us, leaving my clothes crisp and dry. I run a hand through clean hair and grin, Orion blinks rapidly from under fresh glasses. I clap a hand on Novak's shoulder, hoarse voice teasing.

"Your Aether is really something else."

The bard's cheeks warm whilst he presses a fist to his chest and dips his chin for the second time to me. I smile and lower my hand from his slender shoulder, waiting for his wall to slam back up like before. His own happiness does not falter, even when Orion clears his throat. I can deal with Novak's cold walls, if I get moments like this.

"Alvis is right, by that I mean, you're not entirely Water Fae, are you?" Orion pushes up his glasses and I avoid the urge to hit him. Instead I pinch the bridge of my nose, cursing inwardly at his forward question.

My ears perk at the noise from the nearby trading area and I pay interest to the caravan now surrounded by large cabins, already full trade houses swelling with our freshly delivered stocks. Farhaven has a half mile long stretch of road separating the airport from bickering business owners, and the residential village is tucked farther uphill into pines and rocky steppe. We definitely haven't been the only ship here.

"Not sure what else you would call me, but I *am* a Water Fae." Novak says thoughtfully and an orb of crackling water conjures in his freckled hand. I bite my cheek and watch the orb bounce in his hand. Indeed it's filled with water, but also something else …

Almost as if a crackling lightning storm composes the individual molecules of water themselves, akin to the wild blue Aether dancing in his eyes. A gasp of amazement escapes my leathered chest, but Novak doesn't seem to notice. He and Orion are regarding the other, and my brother takes a vial from his belt. I swallow and resolve to knock him senseless later.

"May I?" Orion asks quietly, and Novak's eyes light up.

"Can you find out what I am, exactly?" Novak asks, and I realize some of the crew has stopped to watch us. I step between the two and startle them both, shoving Orion's hand back.

"*No* more science experiments, and certainly not here." I order, and Orion blinks in surprise. Sorrow and shame flows through me and I can't tell whether it's his or mine. Aether study in this fashion is harmless, and I know I've overreacted. I glance sideways to Novak, holding an unreadable expression and his elbows.

"We better get back to work, setting a great example for the crew, aren't we?" I say harshly, then march in the direction of the trading center as opposed to the ship. I can feel Orion staying behind, and I don't hear Novak following. Fine, leave them to it, then.

When I step through the edge of the main square, the last of the stockpiled goods from Farhaven is already loaded onto two wagons pulled by a pair of massive *got*. The beasts are larger than horses with spiraling horns akin to a mountain goat, shagging peppered black coats to match. I give them a wide berth on my way to the center, their hooves twice the size of my head. I decide to continue on and explore on my own, but in all reality my mind is overwhelmed with people and feelings.

I sigh and run a hand through my hair, then quite literally turn in a circle when I reach the residential village as I evaluate the humans go about their day as if a mass murder didn't occur last night. Longhouses let in the fresh warm day, ten foot tall double doors thrown open to reveal hearth fire, song and laughter. A simply made circular gazebo is the second to largest structure in the village, providing an outdoor place to gather.

Women stand on the beautifully manicured plaza of white pebbles surrounding the gazebo and spin wool with dowels laden with a weight, crafting a fine thread as they spread wisdom under the sun to younger generations. Children dart through the village, shouting as they toss a flat disk to each other and are chastised by the full band playing music on the gazebo stage.

I hadn't noticed last night when Orion and I made the obelisk, but we unintentionally nestled the monument between the gazebo and the communal longhouse. I leave the chaos of the main center with my hood up, thankful not to have many stares upon me, and rest a hand on the towering statue composed of fluid crystal. I rest my forehead on the cool surface, and for a moment sound ceases to exist.

What did you two just do?

In all honesty, I don't think either of us knew what would come of our intention, initially our joint thought was to conjure a simple tribute to those we wronged. The Ancient's words from the lake about my abilities haunt me, and I curse myself for being so brash with Novak when he just wants to know what he is. That's what I should be doing, finding out why I'm so strong, even with The Machine snuffing my Aether. I'm just not important enough right now, there will be time.

"It is beautiful, though I can see it cost you dearly." A sharp voice jolts me internally, but on the outside I casually step back from the obelisk. Marta is waiting behind me, dressed in riding breeches and a forest green sweater. The afternoon melt must keep the wolf furs at bay. I dip my chin and press a hand to my chest.

"Well I suppose it's pretty enough, doesn't change the fact they're gone though, does it?" I say and surprise myself with the continued brashness. Apparently, everyone is going to experience my short fuse today. I cross my arms and straighten under her hard glare, gut twisting with red flags.

Her pink lips curve upwards slightly, soft lines along her grey eyes pulling with amusement. She caresses the blue stone beside me, her presence so close rosemary oil flows intensely from her finely plaited hair. Marta doesn't have the same golden and fair beauty as the rest, but a bronzed complexion and light brown hair, common traits similar to those of a Water Fae.

"I have to agree with you." Marta decides after a moment, resting a casual hand on the axe head strapped to her side.

"Hate to say it Chieftess, but that won't do you much good against the likes of me." I muse, brow arched. She chuckles, though her hand doesn't leave the ornate weapon.

"Always a male's way to underestimate a lady. Come, let me give you a tour before your departure. It seems only fitting that a Prince should know what this side of the pond is like." Her hand finally leaves the weapon and reaches for mine. I nod and smile pleasantly, then gesture for her to lead the way. She doesn't miss my rejection, her brows wrinkling slightly, but she plays the role of dutiful host quite well.

I roll over her words in my head, humans don't use the terms male and female, they use man and woman. I make a mental note and walk with the Chieftess, hands clasped behind my back. She points out buildings with protective sigils painted around the doors and details the history of the families who live there or conduct business, and I listen with honest intent. Before long, twilight has blanketed the village.

Lanterns spark to life and humans stop us frequently, chatting with their Chieftess as if she is an old friend. She gives them warm smiles, but falls back into her rigid demeanor as we walk further away from the town under the guise of showing off the distant countryside. We circle around the empty outer edge of the village and face the open farmlands to the north, grand fields tucked beneath mountains. The enormous glacier ranges jut into the clouds, suddenly erupting from nothing.

Marta chuckles and I glance sideways at her, not realizing how far we walked. A meadow now separates us from the village and my gut wrenches. "What?" I ask and casually trace a few steps around her so my back is to the village, and she is closer to the mountain side.

85

"You just have a little bit of drool there." Marta points to my cloak and I stupidly look, drawing another laugh from her.

"Well, I cannot help it if your land is so breathtaking. Truly, you command a wonderful place here Marta, you should be proud." I say and her eyes flicker with delight. She crosses the several paces between us, then rests a hand on my chest. My hackles rise at once and Aether rises to the surface, ready for a fight.

"And do you think *I'm* breathtaking, dear Prince?" She whispers, voice distorted. My brows narrow and I reach for her hand, then pure terror shocks me. A sigil is burned into the skin under her rounded ear, the one covered by her main braid. A binding sigil created long ago, by none other than me.

"No ..." I say through a sudden brain fog, body and mind invaded by her Aether barreling through my useless shields. Her hand leaves my chest and caresses my cheek in a dreadfully familiar way, every muscle is paralyzed by her power while she touches me.

"What's wrong Alvis?" She asks, her glitching face tilted with a pout. I stumble backwards when she releases me, hardly keeping my footing as my mind is further burdened with her malicious intent. Marta cackles and her voice cracks with a familiar demonic giggle. I manage to push her out of my mind and summon a thin violet shield around me, then strengthen my stance after drawing my sword. For a moment, she is out of my mind, but kicking her out depleted my magic greatly, as does keeping her out.

She takes a step forward and sheds her human skin, leaving flesh and brunette hair with every stride. Loyska stands on the other side of my quivering shield, a crazed smile filling her once beautiful face. Scars litter her neck and angled cheekbones, her knee length golden hair catches a gust of wind and twists with manic laughter. Her eyes are no longer silver, irises are replaced by streaks of purple and blue, and the whites are lined with jaundice and popped vessels.

"You're not-"

"Not dead, yes let's skip over the obvious. For one, you're an idiot for thinking your Father would actually kill *me.*" She steps through my shield like a knife through butter and my shield shatters. I raise my sword to her throat, muscles trembling with lack of Aether suddenly stolen from me. Loyska giggles, then snaps her fingers and freezes me in place. She presses a finger to my lips and allows me to keep my voice, a broken nail scraping my skin.

"Spare me the details, let me guess, you're here for revenge." I growl, a sharp snap slices my brain when I attempt to reach Orion. Loyska licks up my neck with a forked tongue, that's new, then bites my ear and tugs. Fur mixes with oily blood on her cracked lips as she pulls away, staring directly into my eyes.

"Dear brother is occupied at the moment," She harshly grasps my cheeks with a skeletal hand. Panic and rage run side by side through my body convulsing in place, if there are more *Nafshyi* here the entire village is in danger. Nails dig into my cheekbones and she smashes her lips onto mine, whispering the rest of her threat as her tongue dives into my throat. "You're not the only one getting yours."

"I swear if you-" I protest under her fatal kiss, earning a slap across my unmovable face.

"What are you going to do Prince? This sigil means nothing now," She lifts her chin to expose the once binding mark between us, "which means I can do whatever I want to you. Though I must say, it was almost too easy. Typhan asked me to wait until the mainland before I showed myself, but I couldn't resist."

I walked right into her trap. All at once she releases my body and I stumble through dizziness, then she pierces my mind as my face connects with the ground. *Yes, not quite the adversary you once were.* Disappointment is apparent in the unwelcome voice in my head, and my fleeting vision disappears entirely.

She screeches, breaking the sky in two as nightmares of Vabel and every person I've ever harmed for Typhan are twisted together, every atrocious act I've ever commited replay over and over in my mind's eye. I drop to my knees, hands over my ears as the sounds of centuries of forced sex and bloodshed echo through my broken soul over and over. Phantom hands tangle through my hair and wander down my chest, my stolen vision makes the sensation even more terrifying as my clothes are ripped off.

"Just get it over with!" I shout, body contorting with physical and mental pain, brain melting into an acidic pulp.

"*Come now, play the game with me. If I don't get my satisfaction from your suffering, I'll have to get it from a certain Zemer.*" She whines, the sound clawing apart my heart as she allows shreds of my vision to return. I shakily stare up at her, Aether dead in my veins and quite alive in hers. Loyska grins, blood dribbling from one corner of her pale cracked lips.

With every ounce of strength I have left I put on a mask of indifference, then spit on her bare feet. "He means nothing to me, and I him."

"Then why is he trying to rescue you?" She asks, caressing my cheek like Father once more. When her skin brushes against mine, the world turns. Disorientation clouds my vision when sharp pain scratches down both my cheeks.

Nauseating warmth streams down my face and I crumple onto my side, squinting at a lone figure in the spinning hazy distance. Blue flames overcome the curling edges of darkness in my vision and I croak out, but Loyska's crackling purple electricity conjures into a whip and wraps around my throat at once. She cackles, separate tendrils of silver teasing my ears before they slip into my mind. I've seen her do this countless times before, destroy people from the inside out, and it's not pleasant.

I decide with certainty I don't want to die anymore, though I'm not left with much of a choice now.

*"Would you like to watch me turn your Zemer inside out first, or have him watch it happen to you **before** I kill him? Oh yes, he looks quite angry, let's do that."* She squeals in my mind like a child, another round of bone snapping pain wrings both my legs and I cry out for the first time, but for an altogether different reason.

"Please don't, do whatever you want to me, but don't hurt him, please." I whisper and she squats beside me, brushing sticky crimson hair from my face. Despite myself, I give her the emotional feast she craves, tears stinging the scratches down my cheeks.

"Anything I want?" She asks, tugging my broken bottom lip with knobby fingers. I nod, swallowing fear. "How pathetic, why didn't you ever care for me this much?"

Loyska smacks me so hard my head meets the muddied ground in an instant, the force pulling on the whip tightening around my neck. My ears ring as she stands and faces a grinning Novak standing ten feet away from us, alone and covered in a dark oily substance.

"I'll thank you to take your hands off what's *mine.*"

Loyska raises a hand to the bard encased in sapphire flames, and hundreds of electrified silver and purple magic missles are launched at him. I scream at him to run but my voice is trapped as I fade in and out of conciseness, pain became a welcome and forgotten sensation long ago. Novak remains still and the attack *bounces* off him, though no shield is visible to my eyes. His dimple filled smile unnerves Loyska and she rages in frustration. I fight against the magic around my neck and look up, catching a glance of her wrinkled brow before she slams me back into the ground with a blast of Aether, leaving my face turned sideways so I can watch.

"Can't say I didn't warn you." Novak taunts, then raises his bare arms overhead, sweater sleeves rolled up. Loyska thrusts both her shaking arms out once more and screams in frustration when her Aether can't find a way inside him. Then, her scream fills with agony and the bonds keeping me in the icy mud are slowly stripped away.

I should be using the opportunity to escape, but am dumb founded by the scene unfolding, and if I'm being honest, a little terrified.

Between Novak's once empty hands is a growing orb of murky water, surrounded by a shield of blue flames. His smile is tightened to a grimace and every muscle flexes in his body, his sweater catches fire as the flames intensify, blinding me if I look directly at him. Silhouettes crest the knoll behind him, Novak's light blocking their features out.

Loyska's body dehydrates rapidly, eyeballs bulge and her paper thin o shaped mouth is hollowed out by a lack of air or moisture. She collapses beside me, body contorted and limbs wrung tight. Silver and purple stares into my soul until her eyes explode with a sickening pop, and I know then she's dead. Water pulls from the atmosphere next, icy molecules slicing past my cheeks as they rush to Novak.

Captain and Orion are at his sides, and he struggles to hold up the swampy orb.

I attempt to push myself to my knees and find out very quickly the bone snapping pain wasn't just an illusion, both my arms and legs are broken. A roaring scream rips through the valley, followed by a howl seconds later from Orion crashing to the ground.

I roll onto my back and stare up at the star filled sky, chaos filling my mind and body as I fade unwillingly into the dark.

Shatter into a million pieces.

"I think you'll like Glen, and Lex, and the townhouse. If you think my music was good before, you should hear me there. All you have to do is wake up." A soft whisper flows beside me, causing my sore ear to twitch. I grimace and move to rub my face, but find my hand entangled with someone else's. I open my eyes reluctantly, quite sure I'm dreaming. Novak is kneeling on the floor at my bedside, my dark hand captured by his freckled one.

A soft smile fills his gaunt face and he releases a long breath. I laugh quietly, then close my eyes and lay my head back.

"I like this dream." I murmur, then fall back asleep.

* * *

Darkness broken by a singular distant lantern waits for me this time when I open my eyes, but I'm still not alone. Novak's hand is in mine, arm stretched at a weird angle as he snores softly on the floor. My arms and legs are no longer broken, and no bandages cover my body. Confusion overwhelms me and I bite my cheek, studying his exhausted features under the dim glow. How long have I been out for?

I close my eyes and focus on finding Orion's presence, locating his sleeping spirit on the other side of the wall my bed rests on. I exhale a breath of relief and begin to remove my hand from Novak's, but he wakes with a gentle startle. I give him a sly smile, then gently tug away from his kindness once more.

Novak bites his lip and soundlessly climbs into the quilt covered bed, settling cross legged beside my sprawled out body taking up half the mattress. Warmth inadvertently flushes my cheeks and neck but I remain still, muscles taut with exhaustion and anticipation. He and I both are dressed in casual sleeping clothes, my plain cream linens contrasting his own soft grey, a color he wears quite often. He and I stare at each other for a moment and I can't fathom why he's so close to me.

"Did I dream that whole thing up, or did you single-handedly bring down my arch nemesis?" I tease, usually deep voice crackling with hoarseness. Nervous laughter fills him, warmth spilling over from his soul to mine. His fingers fidget with the hem of his tunic and my heart flutters seeing him so anxious. Other than the fact he looks thin, there are no after effects from the great amount of Aether he used to face Loyska.

"Do people really have arch nemesis?"

"Well, if anyone has one, it would be me."

"This is true."

I stare at the ceiling, almost more terrified in this awkward silence than when I was moments from death once more. I'm unable to meet Novak's bright gaze burning onto my face, though I do summon courage to find clumsy words. "Thank you, for saving my stupid ass."

"Don't mention it." Novak's hand rests on my shoulder and I turn my attention to him, finding an indescribable expression lighting up his bright eyes, every freckle turned up with happiness. His sapphires light the suddenly minuscule space between our faces as his tight chest presses against mine, warmth radiating from his heart. His lips hover above mine, and he searches my face with wild eyes.

Am I dreaming?

"Wh, what is it?" I ask, breath escaping onto his parted lips in quick pants. Novak's hand slides from my shoulder up my neck, gently tangling with the knotted coils there. I haven't trimmed my hair or jaw in over a week now, and the sensation of his skin on mine is electrifying.

"I," Novak's attention flashes between my lips and violet eyes shining so bright that my light mingles with icy blue shining on his cheeks, "I want to kiss you?"

"Is that a question?" I breathily chuckle, unable to comprehend his body pressed against mine, both our hearts wildly skipping out of control. A brave white vined hand runs up his muscled arm and comes to rest on his freckled cheek.

"I've never been with a male before," He admits, eyes locked onto my soul. My heart drops and I gently push him back, then sit up with weariness and take both his hands in mine. I kiss the top of each set of knuckles and his heart pounds even faster in my ears as my lips leave his skin, confusion drawing his brows together.

"I see. Nova, I most certainly enjoy your company, and I admit I find you quite fascinating, ever since I first laid eyes on your beautiful self, to be exact." Novak's freckled cheeks flush red and my dick twitches, causing me to pull a casual knee up between us, "With that being said, I don't think I should be your first."

Hurt and disappointment spreads across his face, his light brows tightening further to form that worrisome crease. My ears perk as his lungs catch air and pause. I panic as he remains silent and stone faced, resting on his knees beside me.

"I, I just think you deserve someone else, someone who is-"

Freckled hands firmly cup my face and Novak's soft lips meet mine. I melt at once under his touch, as does the crease between his brows. I gently pull him into my lap, his legs settling on either side of me. I lay a deeper passion on him than anyone else in my life, and for a moment I can hear the Ancients singing. In this moment I realize I'm truly in love with him, and I've never loved anyone else like this.

I slip my tongue past his lips, earning a moan from both of us as he gladly dives down my throat. Eagerness drips from his touch, hands desperately exploring my hair and the flexing muscles of my neck. Every part of me he touches is left ablaze and I can't hide my desire anymore, though neither can he. His lips withdraw from mine, only a breaths width away. Novak sighs and grinds himself against me, a shadow of a grin escaping him as my jaw flexes with desire.

"You will be the death of me if you keep moving like that." I murmur, hoarse words more akin to a growl than a seductive whisper.

"*Ai,* who knew you could be so sensitive." His hands leave my hair and travel down my tunic, then he studies every inch of me with a sudden intense seriousness, every flash of his eyes stiffening me further.

"What are you thinking?" I murmur, curious fingers brushing tousled locks from his distracted eyes.

"I have wondered for a long time what it would be like to kiss a male, though I never found anyone I wanted to try with." He mutters, looking up through his blonde lashes reflecting the dim lantern light. I don't know why, but a solid stab to my heart sobers me from the heat of the moment, but I keep an even face.

"Then, why me?" I say, swallowing fear.

Am I nothing more than a handsome body to him, too? If this is all he wants, then I'll find a way to deal with it. At least in this situation I want him too, but not having his heart may break me.

Novak blinks in surprise, breaking from his study of the vines along my neck. "Because I care about you, do you not see that?" He whispers, and tears immediately fill my eyes.

I avert my gaze and fight the emotions bubbling inside me, when that doesn't work I choke on strangled words instead. "You shouldn't."

Novak's small weight leaves me and my veins crawl with disappointment and instantaneous loneliness. I lay on my side and stare at the wall, I can't watch him leave. The lantern clicks off, blankets rustle behind me and a freckled arm slides around my stomach as cold bare feet tangle with mine. He squeezes me tight, forehead nestling in between my broad shoulder blades.

"What, what are you doing?" I ask, still fighting tears begging to be let free.

"I'm tired, and you're warm, is this ok?" Novak murmurs against my tunic, his fluffed ears tickling me.

"Well of course, but I don't understand," I begin, but Novak interrupts with a soft kiss to my spine and blatant words.

"Alvis, you like me, right?"

I still entirely, only burning tears leak out, offering to flood. "To be honest, I think you saved my life the day I met you," I sniff and curse myself under my breath for wretched tears interrupting my confession. "Like is an understatement."

"You know, these tears are not a sign of weakness, they are your strength, your resolve and the pain that has brought you here. To me. I may sound like a selfish jerk, but maybe everything we've been through had to happen, so we could meet,"

Novak inhales sharply and his heart thunders against my relaxing back, "and if I had the choice, I would do it all again, just to meet you. But, it's all done now, and you can let it go. You're allowed to cry, Al."

And just like that, I shatter into a million pieces, and Novak holds me through it all.

* * *

A gentle touch traces down the nape of my neck, between my shoulder blades, then explores down my spine. A content smile fills my face as I register my surprising reality, and I immediately roll over to sweep Novak close to my chest with heavy arms. I feel as if I could sleep forever, but I don't want to miss a second with him.

"I didn't mean to wake you." Novak murmurs, looking up to me with groggy eyes and bruised darkness resting with his freckles. I brush wild hair away from his face and smile, then kiss his forehead.

"I am glad you did, quite a wonderful way to wake up." I rest my chin on his head as he settles against me, a deep sigh heaving from his chest. "Though it seems you didn't sleep much."

"It's your fault, all the rippling muscles and such provoking jealously in this scrawny body of mine." Novak groans playfully and I chuckle, though no heart is behind it.

What he said last night, he really means it, right?

"I did mean what I said last night, I'm not sure what your intentions are, but-" I rake a hand through my hair as he grins up at me, mischievous brow raised while he interrupts with laughter. He rolls over, holding his stomach.

"You make me sound like an evil villain! My intentions." He bellows and I roll my eyes, quietly rising from the bed, back cracking and elbows snapping as my stiff body stretches for what feels like the first time in a week. It probably has been, I've no sense of time and we've been occupied with other things than reality.

"This may be a joke to you, but I've been used since the Spark for my body, Novak. If you need someone to find out what you like with that's fine, I just prefer knowing what I'm getting into, if I can help it." I snap and find a stray cream sweater and replace the sweaty linen I've been wearing with my back to Novak, the sleeves hugging my arms. A shudder threatens to rip me through me and I rub my face with both hands. I can't believe I just said that to him, I didn't mean to reveal so much.

Novak remains deathly quiet behind me and my neck heats further, though I don't know what to say. I glance over my shoulder with fists clenched and spy him seated cross legged on the bed, cheeks carved with tears and eyes cast downwards. I hastily cross the distance between us and kneel on the floor beside the bed, placing shaky hands on either side of him on the mattress. I'm already exhausted from standing.

"I'm sorry, I know you said you cared last night, I should not doubt you, but it's just hard for me. I don't know what's real, everything in my life has had a double meaning." I whisper, the confession draws his glistening eyes up to mine.

"No, don't be sorry. I shouldn't have been so careless, humor is my go to when I'm nervous, and I shouldn't make light of your feelings." Novak rubs his neck and stares at the vines on my right hand for a moment, eyes glazing with deep thought.

"I'm a mess, you know." I tease and study his scrunched up face, sleepy morning looks good on him.

"There's something about you that calls to me, and I don't know how far I want to go, but you," Novak laces his fingers with mine and pulls my hand to his chest with a wet smile, "I don't want to be without you, and saying that out loud sounds crazy, that's why I haven't, but I just-"

I kiss him tenderly and he melts, his hands coming to rest on my shoulders. "It's not crazy, I don't want to be without you, either. I'm here for you Nova, whatever way you'll have me." I murmur onto his lips and he grins under my kiss, a shiver running through him. Novak's lips leave mine to find my now healed ear, then trail across my sharp jawline, breath caressing my throbbing jugular next. I involuntarily growl, dick throbbing with anticipation as his kisses slowly trail back up the other side of my neck.

I want to explore his body, kiss away every worry. I don't care how he wants me, as long as I can have him. Though I would prefer to be behind him, a hand around his throat and the other stroking his cock

97

while my own thrusts inside his perfect body. I would spend days on my knees if that's what he wants, and rapidly changing fantasies course hot desire through me.

"Oh, Nova." I groan, clenching the blankets on either side of him as my shaft springs to life, pressing on my pants. The bard leaves the hollow of my neck, cheeks flushed with delight. I trace his softly angled jaw with a light finger, delighting in how he shivers under my touch. "Do you like it when I call you that, my dear Nova?"

"Yes," He replies breathily, hands tightening on my shoulders, "say it slower, please."

I grip his waist with firm but gentle hands, my body trembling with desire and excitement. I bring my lips to his ear, brushing against his jaw first, then tease the snow fluffed points. I slide a hand up his back and firmly grasp a handful of curls at the base of his neck, tilting his gaze upwards as my teeth graze his throat.

"*No-va.*" I moan with my entire chest against his pulsing artery. I pull back with a fiendish grin, releasing his hair gently as I do so, despite the throbbing ache in my pants. The muscles across his lean chest ripple under his tunic, and his eyes flash upon meeting mine. His fingers desperately hold onto my flexing shoulders for dear life. A hand slides down my shoulder, then my arm, until he finds my fingers wrapped around his hip. His lips open, but no words come out as color rushes his ears.

"Tell me you want this, dear Nova, and I'll take care of you. I promise." I purr, causing his body to tremble under my touch. Just the sight of him so undone has me on edge, pants sticky as I watch his lips open once more.

"I want you, Alvis, I want this." Novak whispers, eyes ablaze with a soft oceanic glow, dimples shining with his handsome smile. I never thought I could come from words alone, but I nearly did right then.

"Good boy." I murmur, then kiss him with reckless abandon as I slide his pants off, fingertips grazing his thighs. I moan in response to his already hard length meeting my hand, core melting at the sensation of his thickness and the idea of him filling me.

No, this isn't about me. He releases a gasp into my mouth as I start stroking slowly with a loose hand, my other hand sliding up his thigh. I lower myself to his cock, thumb firmly brushing over the tip. His eyes widen as he stares down at me.

"Tell me, dear Nova, how do you like it?" I ask, flushing his cheeks a deep red. Blazing eyes connect with my hot gaze and his fingers move to curl my hair. He only bites his lip, nervousness trembling through him. I quicken my pumping and tighten my grip, causing his eyes to roll back in response.

"Like that." He moans, hand twisting further in my hair.

"You sound lovely, don't be afraid to tell me what you want." I murmur, which brings hot stickiness under my quickly working hand. No, he's not coming yet. Pleasure coursing through me begins to throb into pain, and the sound that escapes from him when I take him in my mouth is delicious. He involuntary thrusts deep into my throat, but I anticipated he would. I moan, the vibration mixing with traces of his own pleasure becoming louder but the second.

"*Fuck* ..." He whimpers, attempting to restrain himself. I slide a hand behind his back, pushing him farther down my throat. I stroke his cock in time with my mouth, keeping pressure on his lower back. His hand tightens in my curls as he releases his trepidation, and slender hips thrust him deeper into my throat with reckless movements. I relax my jaw further, relief spilling as he finally takes control. I run my tongue alongside his shaft, gagging inadvertently as the motion drives him harder.

"Wait, wait." Novak warns as his orgasm approaches, he pulls back but I take his hips with both hands, thrusting his warm release deep into my throat. He shudders under me, both hands gripping my shoulders wonderfully tight. I swallow every bit he has to give me, unmoving before I know he's entirely finished. I sit back on my heels and wipe my mouth with the back of my hand, grinning ear to ear.

"You didn't have to do that." Novak's hooded eyes focus on mine with a soft smile, but his brows narrow upon seeing my pants. I crawl onto the bed and lay down, then take his hand and pull him to my chest. I kiss his forehead and ignore the ache rocking my core as I wrap my arms around him.

"I wanted to, and I must say, you taste even better than I thought you would, dear Nova." I tease, releasing a sigh of content. He kisses me deeply, but a wandering hand slides under my pants and takes me by surprise. I carefully catch his wrist and bite my cheek. "You don't have to, let's take it easy."

"I want to feel you, is that okay?" He murmurs on my lips and I release his hand, settling my fingers on his jaw as I gently pull him into another embrace. I gasp when he strokes me through warm stickiness, and his lips turn up in delight against mine. "Glad to know I can take your breath away."

"You have been ever since I met you, dear Nova."

"I'm starting to believe you, my *ahuvi*."

Novak strokes me with a soft grip, uncertainty tainting his lips and motions. Through tender kisses I wordlessly lay my hand over his and show him I like things a little rougher than he does, and he obliges.

"Like this?" He breathes into my lips and I nod, air leaving me in short bursts as his pace quickens, fingers tightening around me. I raise my hips and the hand I once had over his grips his free arm, I want the moment to last but I'm already on the edge from watching him twist with pleasure. Within short minutes I find myself in ecstasy's grasp, unable to hold back any longer. "I'm coming." I warn in a short breath, but he doesn't remove his hand, only quickens his pace.

I drown in his sudden embrace and my heart stops as his soul stares into mine with a dimple filled smile of satisfaction. Hard pumps of release spill warmth onto my shaft and his hand. I dive into his mouth once more, then press my forehead to his, panting heavily.

"By the Ancients Nova, I think I saw stars with that one."

* * *

"Wait, *where?*"

"You know, I'm starting to think there's a reason we call Orion the smart one." Novak teases and I shove his shoulder playfully, in awe of how the morning lights up his curls. Steam curls from our mugs filled with the earthy beverage from Terra, coffee a treat I was not privy to in Sylvan. A week has passed since the incident with Loyska and thanks to the group of female healers who keep to themselves in the red room below, I'm back to my old self.

I want to thank them, but Captain assures me they are aware of my gratitude. In other words, you're the scary prince and they used to be slaves under your kingdom's thumb, stay away. I exhale, raking a hand through my hair as we watch the sun rise in the distance. After spending days tangled in bed with Novak, a new dawn greets our docked ship waiting outside the small trading center of Beakglen.

"I'm not denying that, he's definitely the smart one. I just didn't think *'headquarters'* was really in the middle of Hallowed. Will Captain stay with the ship again?" I gesture around us to the still sleepy ship. Captain lingers at the helm with Orion as some of the crew wanders around with coffee and disgruntled grogginess, waving to me and Novak as they walk by.

"Nay, this is the only place she'll leave her ship." Novak says, surprising me. I watch my brother talking to Captain, Orion has been attached to her by the hip, apparently he's next in line if something happens to her, not Novak, so he's been attentive in his crash course on how to sail.

Captain seems to have a funny way of doing things.

"Morning brother, enjoy your last few days?" Orion asks in earnest and I send him nothing but love across the bond, and a hint of sarcasm. *"Besides almost dying, yes they were rather wonderful."* I tease, drawing silent laughter from him. He continues on with Captain and I focus on Novak, who has been waiting patiently, must be my face 'went funny' again. My cheeks flush and I finish the rest of my coffee, delighting in how it warms my soul. My brows narrow and I stare into my cup.

"What's on your mind?" He asks and I leave my mug beside his on a rickety barrel stood up on end by the main mast, then leave the center of the ship to lean on the railing facing the town. I overlook the sea of golden and pink clouds above, briefly wonder what the village of Beakglen on the horizon is like, mind spiraling for a moment as I try to figure out what's wrong.

Novak leans beside me, cloaked shoulders touching, and tangles his fingers with mine on the railing. He glances sideways at me a few times, but waits for me to speak. After a few minutes, I figure out exactly what's bothering me.

"I'm happy Nova, and that scares me." I whisper as we watch the clouds change colors together.

"Because you feel like you don't deserve to be, or because something bad will happen?"

"Both, I suppose." I decide and he nods, contemplating his next words very carefully.

"Do you want to know when I started to figure out you weren't the bad guy?" I stare at him, blue eyes still soft and inviting as he rocks back on his heels. After a moment I nod, voice choked with fear.

"The way you treated that Fae, the one in my cell. If you were like the rest of your family, you wouldn't have spoken to him, let alone given him your cloak." He declares at once with a smile, then begins plucking imaginary bits from the air dramatically. "I found bits and pieces of you, the real you, and when you put them all together, you're quite extraordinary yourself."

I stand and face him at once, tears relentlessly streaming down my cheeks. Novak straightens and rests careful hands on my shoulders, soft honesty emanating from his warm smile. "Thank you, I needed to hear that."

"Nothing by the truth." He says, then throws his arms around me. I bend down and bury my face in his neck and hold him tight, then the thought crosses my mind we shouldn't be embracing on the main deck. I stiffen and he senses my worry, reluctantly releasing me. "I'm not hiding this, I hope you know that."

I laugh, ruffling his honeyed hair upon straightening. "I'm not scared, *Zemer*."

"Hate to interrupt you lovebirds, but I need Novak." Captain announces, arriving with Orion beside him. She smiles at me and I bow my head. "Glad to see you're alive."

"Glad to be alive." I say and Novak takes me by surprise by kissing my cheek, then him and Captain leave us for her quarters.

"Well, that escalated quickly." Orion taunts and I grin, rubbing my neck nervously. "Goodness, you look like me, what has that boy done to you?"

"Oh, knock it off." I elbow him softly, though I can't argue with him very much. "Any idea what the plan is?"

"Yeah, Captain decided we're going to stay for a week, vacation or something like that." Orion says, sunlight glinting off his dirty glasses.

"She can just leave the ship here that long?" I ask, blinking rapidly.

"According to her, she has license to dock where she pleases from the High Lady herself. They literally make their own dock, wherever they go. If you weren't *occupied* last night you would've been able to watch the Earth Fae create the scaffolding."

103

I glance at Orion, wondering what feeling is crossing over his glazed eyes. I try to give him privacy if something isn't obvious, but I feel like something's been off since I yelled at him in Farhaven. "Well, her and Novak both are free spirits, that's for sure." I decide, not sure what to say to diffuse the odd thick air around us.

"I'm glad he makes you happy." He chuckles, tying his meddlesome inky hair in a knot at the base of his neck, though tendrils still fly around his face. A sudden urge to hug him crosses over me and I do so at once, surprising him and me. "What's wrong?" He asks, returning my embrace.

"Nothing, I just love you, O. You know that, right?" I say, arms tightening around him.

"Of course I do, you brat."

Headquarters.

"Welcome to Beakglen." Novak proudly announces as we approach the outskirts of the quaint village already bustling with life first thing in the morning.

The streets are wide here, freshly cobbled with great care and precision, no bumps or uneven spots in the road. Children run alongside our caravan of pirates, instantaneously recognizing the *Zemer* with glee. Captain has opted for a subtle entrance, leaving her hat behind and hiding her unmistakable hair and eye combination under a thick black cloak as she walks in the center of our group. A crisp breeze sweeps through the streets and makes me wish I added another layer under my clothes, the air chills me much more since we left Silverbury.

Chants of 'Will you play?' interrupt our journey to the infamous headquarters located on the northeastern edge of town, though Novak takes it all in stride. I've noticed the smile he gives others isn't the same as the one I earned from him last night, and the thought quickens my pulse. Orion clears his throat beside me and I straighten, ignoring Novak's confused stare as the three of us lead the way. The healers decided to stay on the ship, though they're free to leave any time, and the small Air Fae follow Captain.

"Have you ever been here?" Captain quietly asks behind me and I fall in step with her, leaving Orion with Novak at the front. The eldest child tugs my cloak and I glance over my shoulder, throwing her a soft smile. The smaller children walking alongside her brighten upon seeing my friendly face, and I wonder why they aren't scared of me.

"No, smaller villages." I turn my attention to Captain, explaining my travels in as few words as possible. She nods, and as I look around the town filled with Air and Earth Fae, a thought comes to mind. "Why here?"

"Well, it's central to everything, and Hallowed was the first land I started business in, besides Iron, of course. The master of arms before you built 'headquarters' after he retired, as our dear first mate calls it."

"Is that so? Novak's told me quite a few stories about him, Lexeran, right?"

"*Ai*, he's always been fond of the old man. Lex practically raised us, after the incident."

"Incident?" I ask, brows raised. Novak giggles ahead of us, as do several of the crew members around us. Captain chuckles but darkness haunts her eyes, a familiar facade to hide pain.

"You haven't heard that one, eh?" She asks me, perking Orion's ears ahead of me. I shake my head. "Perhaps Novak will tell the tale tonight then, how I became Captain."

"Sure thing, Cap." Novak agrees, and we continue walking in gentle conversation. Novak is a wonderful tour guide, he knows everyone here and points out various tall buildings constructed of wood and brick, though every word he tells me about them is lost in a blur. Does he distract me this much after such a short time together?

"Alvis, I swear to the Ancients, get your shit together before I get a headache." Orion removes his glasses and rubs his face, outwardly ignoring me my stare he berates me. Before I can think of something clever we've turned onto the a quaint street bordering the countryside and Captain

points out the tallest building at the end of the street.

"Welcome to Headquarters." She says, and warmth washes over my soul to see people waiting outside the place. Even though I don't know them, a strange feeling fills me upon seeing warm smiles waiting for our group. As we approach however, warmth is replaced by sheer panic and my heart beats suddenly out of control.

Orion stops walking and I stumble into him, cursing under my breath. Captain touches my arm and I shudder, so she drops her hand. It takes me precious seconds to realize this feeling isn't mine, my brother is trembling in front of me owns these terrifying emotions so intense my heart is wracked with pain.

"*What's wrong?*" I ask as I push back on his feelings and regain my breath, then stand by his side. Novak waits with worry along his brows at our state and when Orion doesn't respond, I follow his gaze to Captain pulling a short hazel haired male into a tight embrace. I glance between the male and Orion as his heart beats faster, pounding in my ears.

"*I, I don't know.*" He stutters across the bond, staring at the male laughing at Captain. I bite my cheek and hide a grin, then loop my arm through both Orion and Novak's. I peer sideways at Novak and find him smiling, must be Orion's feelings are so apparent Novak can tell without a bond Orion just fell in love.

* * *

The townhouse is two stories of pure warmth and cozy welcome, chatter flows from the dining and living rooms neighboring each other and I work in the modest sized kitchen beside Emeric, the Fae who sends my brother's heart into a flutter. The kitchen is surrounded by floor to ceiling windows on the back and right wall, a counter island separates us from the dining room and a cook stove rests along the other side wall.

Plants hang in clay pots, suspended by macrame knots along all the windows and line the other places of the house I've been through so far. The space is lightly decorated with the paraphernalia of a bookworm, perhaps even a writer. In the kitchen, cast iron and steel reign, along with a rolling butcher block in the center of Emeric's tidiness.

I stir the quickly thrown together rabbit and root vegetable soup boiling in a massive steel pot on a wood stove while he finds more bowls. Our company is larger than he expected but that's no problem, as he's repeatedly assured me. He's another untypical Fire Fae, his skin is dark brown and his sleek chin length hair matches his complexion. I admire his finely cut green tunic cuffed at his wrists, his soft figured dressed in simple classic beauty. Novak's laugh cuts through the rest and I smile whilst dimming the fire.

"How are you liking the ship?" Emeric asks, handing me a bowl.

"I've taken to flying quite nicely, I figured I would be more air sick than I have been." I chuckle and he grins, the muscles in his square jaw flickering. "And why do they leave you here, eh? You're quite impressive company."

Emeric takes the bowl I've filled and sets it on the island counter, the steaming meal quickly snapped up by hungry hands. He hands me another and I fill it again, his deep red eyes flickering. "I prefer the quiet life, Captain is horrible with numbers and paperwork, so I take care of that for her, and the house." He says quietly, and I nod.

"I envy you, I wouldn't know how to sit still."

"You must've sat still long enough at some point to learn how to cook like this, you were in the kitchen for only ten minutes after coming back with all those rabbits, *and* you put together an entire meal that smells better than anything I've ever had." We trade bowls once again and his eyes cast downwards. "You all arrived sooner than I anticipated, otherwise I would've had it made already … "

"Don't fret, I enjoy cooking, it's one of the few ways I could rebel against my father, my friend and I started a soup kitchen of sorts for the slaves and lower class when we were only a few decades old, having to use scraps so no one noticed, not to mention it still had to *taste* good."

"You did that?" Novak asks, leaning on the island with Captain and Orion at his sides. I drop the empty bowl Emeric had just handed me, but the Fire Fae is quick and saves the fine white ceramic before it shatters.

"Surprised, *Zemer*?" I throw over my shoulder, focusing on taking the bowl from a calm Emeric.

"Not at all." He says and I hand him a hearty portion, his fingers brush mine as he takes the bowl from me. My heart skips and I bite my cheek, smiling half heartedly. I steal a glance at Orion, finding him staring at me with a sad smile. He knows now, the punishment for those 'crimes' I commited with Charis. I was forced to violate her while Typhan watched, the other option was for him to take her maidenhood while I watched, but she wouldn't have that.

We were both punished for rebelliousness my friends approve of, the fire in their eyes sparking as they see more proof of the good I tried to accomplish in my hell. I avoid Novak's eyes and continue to work with Emeric, burying my half truths deep inside my heart as I focus on the oblivious happiness flowing around me.

It's not long before everyone is fed and I take my meal outside. Emeric leads me to the backyard and we escape the overwhelming chaos inside. A split rail fence lines the expanse, frost bitten grass separated by softly rolling hills. Several stone benches rest in the center around a fire pit, but the yard is otherwise empty. The mid afternoon sun barely warms me against the chill, the sweat on my brow turning cold within a few minutes. Emeric and I eat in silence, overlooking the land beyond.

"Captain found me in Obsidivale when I was in my seventy sixth year, I found out later it was her first time visiting the Court since she was a child." Emeric stares into the distance and I glance at him sideways, listening patiently. "Did you know they have slaves there, too?"

"I assumed, I know they're quite a rich High Court, though I've never been there. I've only encountered the occasional Fire Fae in the mainlands and hear second hand from them."

Emeric nods, his orange eyes darkening as he contemplates his next words.

"From a young age I was sold into slavery, and after the Spark I became Visha's personal harlot. He's a vicious beast, and … Well, I fought back against my master too many times." Emeric glances sideways to me with a sly grin tainted by trauma. "When Captain found me, my neck was stretched beneath an axe blade. Rebellious slaves were unfathomable to the High Lord and after the uprising two centuries ago, he began public executions in the main square."

"What happened next?" I ask, arms crossing as I face him, fully captured by his tale.

"She was already famous for what happened to her father's ship and her work in Hallowed, so when the legendary Captain set the chopping block on fire and demanded to purchase such a beautiful slave five times what he was worth, Visha couldn't refuse. There is one thing he loves more than reputation, and that's money."

Emeric's eyes never leave mine as he tells his story, his dimpled chin raised. "*But*, as you might've guessed, ships and I don't mix, so she gave me my freedom and a place to stay, a purpose besides satisfying others."

I rest a hand on his shoulder, my brows drawn together. "Thank you for sharing your story with me, but I have to ask. Why are you telling me this?"

"Earlier, I saw the light leave your eyes after Novak said that. I just know what it's like to have memories haunt you, and how it can be easier to let them do so rather than face your demons with others. Novak's a good male, he'll listen, or Captain, or me. We're all your family now. Your brother too, you can see the way he cares for you."

Thick tears fall down my cheeks and I press my forehead to Emeric's, heart split wide open. "Thank you." I stupidly mutter, because what can you say to all that?

The back door is thrust open, Novak and a giant Fire Fae step outside and pause open seeing Emeric and I. I wipe my eyes with my sweater sleeve and recompose myself, Emeric takes my bowl and bows his head, nodding to the Fae with Novak before retreating inside.

"You alright?" Novak asks, hands fidgeting. I nod, turning to face him and his ginger bearded companion.

"You must be Lexeran, I'm Alvis." I press a fist to my chest and bow to the weathered old Fae, wrinkles turn up his proud orange eyes as he gives me the same show of respect.

"*Ai*, hopefully whatever you've heard are all good things." Lex chuckles in a deep baritone, rustling Novak's hair which only comes up to the crimson cloaked Fae's waist. Novak beams as he pushes Lex's scarred hand away.

"Of course, anyone who can wrangle Captain and this one are good in my book." I tease, drawing laughter from Novak and Lex both. "Where is she, anyway?"

"I've brought a new recruit from the Mists, a Wild Fae who wants to learn the ropes of flying an airship. Her and Captain are discussing inside."

"Great, another rookie who thinks they can fly." Novak rolls his eyes, earning a swat upside the back of the head. I snicker, a soft breeze lifting my hair and Novak's. Lexeran's bright red is cut short, but his thick beard reaches his chest.

"Umber isn't a rookie, she's a good friend of mine so you better watch it."

"Sheesh old man, when you'd get so cranky?" Novak shoves the immovable boulder of a Fae, and I smile watching the two.

111

"Since you've caused all these gray hairs." Lexeran retorts, stroking his beard speckled with curled silver. Laughter rolls in our direction as the crew makes their way outside, though Orion and Emeric are missing. Skin prickling anxiety crawls over me as the yard fills with people, though I'm glad Orion is talking with the kind Fae.

Emeric knows nothing about me other than I'm the Prince of Sylvan and all the rumors and ugly truth that goes with that fact, yet he still offered his ear and friendship to me. In my opinion, he's perfect for Orion, and the male truly gave me courage. Novak's hand finds mine and startles me, mind lost in a daze.

"Hey, wanna get out of here?" He asks and I raise a brow.

"Captain probably won't be happy if you bail on your own party." I counter as Lex brings a bonfire to life in the stone pit, our companions gathered close around it. Captain hugs Lexeran tight, having to stand on her tip toes so she can wrap her arms around his thick neck.

"Nah, we'll be alright. I have something I want to show you." Novak admits, fingers tightening around mine as his cheeks flush against the cold. I pull his woolen hood up over his head, then brush hair away from his bright eyes. Without thinking, I dip my lips down to his and tenderly kiss him. A second later I pull back but he smiles, leaning into me.

"I thought you weren't scared."

"I'm not." I say, returning his happiness.

Levaya.

⟋⟍⟋⟍

We walk back to the dimly lit ship guarded by a few crew members and continue our journey beyond it, traveling through a small grove of oak trees. Gentle conversation fills the late afternoon spiked with overpowering sun rays slowly trapped by the horizon in the west. Novak's hand hasn't left mine since we snuck away from the house, and I'm grateful for his warmth.

"How much longer?" I ask, whining pathetically.

"Almost there, are you tired?" Novak asks earnestly, slowing his step through icy leaf litter hidden from the sun by the naked trees towering hundreds of feet above us.

"Not really, I just like giving you a hard time." I say, though I really am exhausted. I can't bring myself to admit it though, I spent a week in bed after Farhaven and sleeping is the last thing I want to do.

"Well, you're certainly good at that." He teases, giving me a sideways smile. As the quiet wood darkens the further we travel, tiny floating lights catch my attention in the break of trees ahead of us. I stumble on a root and Novak steadies me, giving me a 'yeah right you're not tired' look, but I can't argue as the full reality of the place we've entered hits me.

The clearing holds a small pond with a thin sheet of ice blanketing it's luminescent bright blue water. Fireflies with gold and silver lights dance over the ice and into the night sky, dancing under the half moons hanging over our slice of paradise. The small area is surrounded by grand oaks, maples and evergreen bushes, making me feel as if we've entered a whole separate world.

"Aren't fireflies only a summer thing?" I ask, I've only seen them myself a few times.

"*Ai*, though these ones never leave, despite the weather."

"Beautiful." I breathe, staring at the dancing lights that match the moons above.

"Believe it or not, I like to be alone most of the time. Captain showed me this place the first time she brought me here, and I can't visit Glen without spending some time here. Makes my heart feel better." Novak explains and I turn my head to find him watching me with a soft smile.

"I take it you noticed I'm not a fan of crowds?" I mutter.

"Is anyone?" He replies, and I shrug. I stand behind him and wrap my arms around his waist, and he rests his hands on mine over his stomach.

"Thank you, I needed this."

We stand like that for a long time, watching the fireflies reach into the sky and dive back down to the ice in the impossibly gold twilight. Owls and other animals slowly come out from their hiding places, the natural music of the wood resuming as we remain still. Two white foxes make an appearance, dancing around the water's edge as they scurry through the place. I chuckle watching them and a sigh of content leaves me.

"Oh, there's one more thing." Novak says, twisting in my arms so he's facing me. His lashes are frosted over and I frown, wishing I could warm him. He reaches into his coat pocket hiding under his cloak, first retrieving a small white jar with lavender flowers painted along it's surface. He reaches back in with his other hand, pulling out a leather corded necklace with a wooden anchor at the end.

Novak holds them both up to me with chattering teeth and I take the necklace first, studying the fine craftsmanship. Impossibly detailed ropes snake around the anchor, and a sword is engraved along the stem of it. "What are these for?" I ask, smiling.

"Well, that there I made while waiting for you to wake up after we left Farhaven. Captain said I was going to pace a hole in the deck so I kept my hands busy." Novak's freckled cheeks flush further, though I don't think it's from the cold. My smile broadens and I slip the necklace on, clutching the anchor tight. "I was going to wait until Yule, but I figured now's a good time as any."

"You made this, for me?" I reaffirm and he nods with a small satisfied smile, then offers the jar which is surprisingly heavy and fits in the palm of my hand. I tilt my head, studying the flowers. "Don't tell me you made this too."

Novak laughs, though his smile fades. "No, I didn't. I don't know if you have *levaya* in Silverbury, but I thought you might like to bury this here, on the mainland where you can visit. After you and Orion built that obelisk, there were ashes surrounding it." Novak rubs his neck nervously. "This jar was the first thing I could find, some lady gave it to me, and I put some of the ashes inside. A part of your mother, I figured."

"*Levaya?*" I ask, staring into his eyes as my fingers wrap around the jar.

"Right, sorry, *levaya* means funeral rites. Where I'm from there are a few prayers in the old language said as we bury our dead, we wish them well in the next place and celebrate their life. I've always liked it that way, celebrating inside of mourning. I can show you, if you want." Novak kicks a chunk of ice as I silently take the jar from him, tears threatening to freeze onto my cheeks as I tuck it away into a safe inner pocket of my own jacket.

Winter catches in my lungs as I stare down at this wonderful male and I wait for the universe to take away my happiness. He's too good to be true, the consideration and kindness I've received from him though I've brought him nothing but pain, mends my cold heart. Until I lose this love I do not deserve, I will drown myself in it.

"Nova, I love you." I admit, dipping my lips down a breath away from his. "I know that's an impossible feeling to have after such a short time, but I feel as if you're the reason I was put on this earth."

Novak's arms encircle my neck and he kisses me fiercely, his mouth warming me from the chill and the centuries long permafrost that has encapsulated my heart. "Let's go home, we'll come back tomorrow for the *levaya*." He murmurs into my lips, the word home sending flutters through my stomach.

* * *

We crash into Novak's room in the ship, nearly ripping the blue tapestry off the door frame as we push through in a flurry of hungry hands and lips. I undo his cloak and he mine, then he stands on his toes once more to kiss me again. I chuckle against his mouth, causing his brows to narrow and head to tilt.

"What's so funny?"

"You're just so short compared to me is all."

Before I can tease any further, Novak shoves me onto the bed and I land onto my back with surprise filling my wide eyes as he leaps on top of me, legs straddling either side on the mattress. "Who's the short one now, fucker?"

"Apologies, sir." I attempt to sit up but he pushes me down with a firm hand, mischief playing across his dimples as he removes layers from his torso. "In a hurry?"

"Is that a bad thing?" Novak asks through short breaths, fingers

116

trailing the numerous hems of my jacket, sweater and under layers resting across my waist.

"Not at all, I'm just curious what you plan on doing to me." I whisper, chest vibrating with the primal tone he enjoys. His hands slide under my clothes which I desperately want off, but I let him enjoy his fun as my violet eyes flash, lighting up the dark room along with his own glowing bright blue. "Other than torturing me." I groan, earning the privilege of layers slipping over my head, his heated fingers brushing against my taut chest and shoulder muscles.

"I want to do what you did to me." Novak murmurs into my ear, grinding himself against my stiff cock and taking my breath away. Despite spending the day and night together in bed, we've still only had the one experience, but I enjoy laying with him and feeling his body under my hands, studying every inch of him. "Can I?"

"You can do whatever you want to me." I run my hands up his bare back, receiving a shudder underneath my touch as I trace one up his neck, dark fingers tangle in his hair. His lips find mine and he kisses me with surprising softness, though his sparking eyes and eager dick tell a different story.

"That's a broad statement." Novak mutters as his mouth leaves mine and trails down my neck, then the center of my chest. His fingers grasp my pectorals and I moan, driving my hips upwards as his lips meet my hard stomach.

"I trust you." I say, immediately jolting Novak's attention up to me, pausing his hands working at my pants. I caress his cheek and smile, receiving a kiss on my palm before I retreat and rest both my hands behind my head.

Novak doesn't waste any more time, I expect him to be shy but the moment I'm sprung free from the confining fabric he takes me in his hand and I inhale a short gasp. His hand is warm, delicate fingers tighten as he explores up and down my shaft, where all of his attention is diverted. I stare down at Novak with a sly smile, not having to wonder long what his mouth will be like.

He starts slow, mouth encircling halfway down my twitching cock before he revisits the tip, tongue encircling the head. I groan and my left hand immediately finds his hair, though I corral my need to play rough and only gently tousle his locks in my fingers. "You're quite good for someone who hasn't done this before." I manage and he pulls his mouth away from me for a moment, saliva connecting his lips to my cock.

"I'm new, not an idiot." Novak says with a raised brow and wicked grin before resuming his work, but he can't make it any farther than he did before. His brow furrows with frustration and I hold back the urge to thrust into his mouth, he's not ready.

"Relax, you don't have to take me all." My words only spur determination and he gags, tongue diving farther along the underside of me. "Relax your throat and jaw, you won't get anywhere like that." He obliges and slows his pace, putting intention behind his motion. As his lips near the bottom of my aching shaft, he takes my hips and drives me further into his throat.

"Fuck!" I moan, fingers inadvertently yanking his hair as I press his head down. He groans in delight around me. "Is this what you want?" I ask, and he replies with removing his mouth from me, bringing his wet lips to my own.

"Show me more, how else does it feel good?" Novak asks, eyes gleaming as he stares into mine with a wild racing heart. I take his face in my hands, air leaving me in quick bursts.

"I'm warning you, this won't be quick like before. I need you."

"Show me, please." He asks, and I oblige.

We settle ourselves further up on the bed and Novak is kneeling between my legs, oil in one hand and leaking cock in the other as he strokes himself. He watches me prepare myself for him with an oiled finger, then another as my other hand works myself. I've never felt this comfortable in this situation before, and certainly never done it with someone I've cared about so much. Will it feel different?

"Does it hurt?" Novak asks, slender muscles in his arms and shoulders brimming with anticipation, his free hand trails up my thigh to meet my fingers. I moan and arch my hips, the sensation from his confident touch is soul shaking.

"Sometimes, but most of the time, if you're careful like this," I manage to breathe out, then replace the fingers inside me with his own curious ones, and he doesn't flinch when he enters, "It helps." I moan the last two words and my shaft twitches under my hand, insignificant warmth spilling from the top as he becomes comfortable with his pace.

"Like this." I invite him to curve his fingers and find *the* spot, then bite my cheek to avoid smiling at his cute, if determined clumsiness.

"I'm still afraid I'll hurt you." Novak says, but I recognize that carnal fire in his eyes and I can see how undone he is watching me writhe underneath him. My sticky hand wraps around his throat and he stares me directly in the eyes, fingers pausing inside me as my grip tightens.

"Fuck me, Nova. I want you, and I'm ready."

My tight embrace around his throat and lewd words immediately unleash a beast, erasing all traces of the shy male I've encountered thus far. Novak's fingers are quickly replaced by the tip of him pressing against me. His eyes flash to mine and he licks his lips, waiting for me with impatience brewing in his tightening fingers.

Fuck, I can't come yet.

"Please." Is all I have to say, and he slips inside me with a delicious growl rocking his chest. A strangled groan leaves me, darkness curls the edges of my vision as he teases his length deeper and deeper, but not all the way. I lift my hips up in attempts to get closer, but he arches a brow. The hands around my hip and neck are wonderfully firm, taking away my control.

"Good boy." I hoarsely say under his grip, throat bobbing as I grin wickedly and move my hand to the nape of his neck, yanking his face closer to mine and driving him deeper. "Now, try and hurt me." I ask, then bite his lip so harsh I draw blood. I hope I didn't misjudge that look in his eye as his hand leaves my throat.

"As you wish." Novak slides my one of my legs over his shoulder, grinning as I clutch the blankets around me and flinch at the subtle movement inside me. Every muscle in my body is rigid with desire while awaiting him to make good on his word, one his hands settles underneath me and lifts me slightly for a better angle, the other holds my leg firmly in place, fingers digging into my thigh.

"I'm curious, does it really feel that good, where the slightest movement makes you look like that?" He slowly draws his hips back and forth, pumping gently inside me and careful to never leave.

"Mm, like what?" I ask, eyes hooded as my hands explore his stomach, then his chest. He's so fucking beautiful, how did I get so lucky? Suddenly, he's no longer slow and sweet.

Once gentle hands firmly hold me in place as he rails me, thrusting into me so hard the headboard slaps against the wall. I cry out in pleasure and pain when he buries himself entirely inside me, my hands desperately cling to his lower back as he remains paused like that for a moment, so deep I can't move even if I wanted to.

"Promise me something." He whispers into my fluffed ear, causing it to flicker as he thrusts once more.

"Anything."

"From now on, I'm the only one who can make you feel this way. Your face is only allowed to twist with pleasure from me, and you can only smile at me in that way you do when we're together." Novak is serious, eyes crackling with icy blue and lighting the darkness between our faces as he stares into my soul.

"I've been yours since the moment we met, don't worry." I murmur, but his face darkens. He withdraws from me and confusion settles, then is quickly replaced by heat when he grabs me by my hips and turns me over so he's behind me. Novak enters me again with less hesitation and slips an arm around my chest, then pulls me back so my back is flush to his front.

"Nova!" I cry out, he's so fucking big and this angle makes me feel full. I shudder under the overwhelming sensations, unable to escape the pleasure lighting me on fire.

I've never been held this way before, but I want more.

"That's not good enough. Try again." Novak says, his free hand takes my cock as he thrusts slowly inside me. We're back to making love now. I reach back and find his hair, then gently pull his lips down to my shoulder where he bites with no mercy.

Mmm, or a wonderful mix of sex *and* love.

"Yours, only yours, and you are mine, only mine." I murmur, voice filled with desperate pleasure as climax nears. Novak's thrusting turns faster as I struggle to speak once more, the arm around my chest secures me as the hand around my shaft quickens. "Only you make me feel this way, Nova, only you."

"Only me, only you." He kisses the hollow of my neck and fucks me like a wild animal, relentlessly taking me after my confession. "Can I?" He asks, climax building inside me and him.

"Please." The strangled word is all I can say, but it's enough. Warmth spurts from me, landing onto his hand and the bed below as my world shifts on it's axis. My ears ring as the hand around my chest slides up to my neck, holding me tighter against his body as he releases deep inside me with strong thrusts, and gorgeous moans escape into my ear.

"Alvis, I love you." Novak admits and color flushes my cheeks as my cock comes to attention at his words, despite having just came. "I didn't want to say it before just because you said it, but I do, love you."

"Love me again." I ask, and he gently kisses my cheek.

"No, this time I want you to love me."

III

Insanity

It's Nova.

⚜

Okucha, High Court of Borealis
16,075 A.C , One Year Later

I sling an arm around the back of Novak's chair, laughter echoes through the spacious tavern lit by an array of floating lanterns as he wildly tells the story of how he knocked me out in the Shipwreck. I fidget with the satchel in my pocket with my other hand, watching my lover with pure content rolling through my soul. Yule is coming and I planned on asking Novak then, but I can't wait any longer. The past year on the ship has been the best in my entire life, and I think the same can be said for Orion.

With some nudging from me and a few more visits to Beakglen, Orion realized the heart attack he suffered upon meeting Emeric was due to infatuation indeed, and the two have been lovers for quite some time now. Umber joined the crew and put Novak's worries of having a rookie on the ship at ease, she's been infinitely useful with insider information and working as a deckhand. Lexeran makes an appearance from time to time in Glen when we're there, though something happened between him and Captain during our visit two

125

months ago that she won't talk about.

"To be far, I wasn't knocked *entirely* out, just *mostly* out." I muse before taking a drink and Orion shoves my shoulder with a grin, seated at my right alongside the stretching beer filled table. Novak chuckles and rests a hand on my left thigh, squeezing tight.

"Drink another and we'll reenact it for 'em, been awhile since we had a good scrap." Novak teases, his cheeks flush at once when I wink at him and lace my fingers with his on my leg. Whistles and catcalls emit around the table from our crew, furthering my wicked grin as I lean over to whisper in Novak's ear.

"You sure about that? Last night *and* this morning was-" Novak jolts upright in his chair as if struck by lightning. Our table is silent and I quickly glance around, finding nothing out of the ordinary except every face out of the dozen at our table is set on Novak's wide eyes. The sea salt scent I've come to fall asleep with and catch glimpses of during the day heightens until it's all I can smell, and when I follow Novak's starstruck gaze, my heart stops.

A small female is seated at the bar across the room from us, light blue eyes flashing whilst locked onto Novak. Air is non-existent and something unspoken is occurring between them, Novak's fingers tighten around mine as his eyes flash in return, dual sparkling oceans matching that of the female's. Heat swells down my neck and my palms sweat, the multitude of wool layers I have on were combating the freezing cold of Borealis, but now I'm soaking through each one as Novak's trance continues. Fae and Humans around the table quietly begin talking once more, and they're no longer staring at Novak.

I'm sorry, Alvis." I shoot a death glare to Orion who is solemnly packing my long handled pipe on the table, eyes down. Everyone is staring at me now, and the room spins as I try to find air, but it's too thick and slippery. I release Novak's hand, breath leaving me shakily, and he snaps out of it. Novak shakes his head and a soft smile returns to his face, his hand finds mine before I go too far and he squeezes tight.

The crew commences like nothing ever occurred, and thankfully Umber obnoxiously requests Nova to play and he heads for the stage, swiping his lute from the table with furrowed brows betraying his half hearted smile. The blue skinned Fae takes his empty seat and slides a mug full of mead over to me. "What're you gonna do now?"

"Nothing, nothing's going to happen." I scowl at her and drink the entire mug, slamming the empty cup down with too much force. The blonde female is still alone at the bar, watching Novak with intensity. She doesn't look like anything special, a plain long sleeved black dress is nearly hidden by layers of plaid shawls and several furs, and her short pointed ears fold down the moment Novak begins playing, dismay creeping across her round face. She doesn't like his music?

Umber grunts, swinging her legs up and crossing her ankles on the edge of the table, her body facing away from me as she watches Novak revive the drunk crowd back to life as the midnight hour chimes on a tall clock in a corner of the smoke filled room. "If you think he's just going to get back on the ship after finding his mate, you're dumber than I thought."

Usually Novak's music calms me instantly, no matter the mood, but I can only watch the female size up Novak for five minutes. I stand up so quickly my rickety chair is thrown back, and I march for the front door. I make the stupid mistake of looking over my shoulder before stepping into the dusky street. The female has left the bar and is approaching Novak who is attempting to get through the crowd keeping him from me. His eyes lock with mine, oblivious to his mate right behind him, and I dart into the night.

* * *

Per usual, Captain is the only one left on the ship. I stand outside her cabin with fists clenched and heart thrumming. I raise a hand and before I can knock, she opens the door. I blink, surprised to see her without her full leather and lace regalia. Raven hair is tied back in a loose knot off to the side, and she's only wearing a long night shirt. A once hidden tattoo of a grey lion stretches down her right thigh and I blush, stepping backwards.

"Oh stop and just get in here, I assume someone's dying." Captain steps out of the way and gestures for me to come in.

"No one's dying." I mutter, then shove my hands in my pockets and pace to her desk, taking a seat in the high backed chair while she pulls a loose pair of trousers on.

"And you're still standing, yet it's only midnight. What happened?" Captain perches on her desk in front of me, feet dangling and glowing red eyes focused on me. I bury my face in my hands, elbows on my knees as tears burn my throat and face. Captain jumps up and kneels on the floor between my legs, her hands prying mine from my wet cheeks. "Alvis, what's wrong?"

"It's Nova, I think he found his mate."

Silence echoes and I'm lost in Captain's eyes flashing every shade of orange, pink and red possible. Her face is unreadable, save for a small crease between her angled brows. I don't know what I expect her to say, after all Novak is essentially her brother, of course she would be happy for him. I sniff and lean back in the chair, pulling from Captain's grasp. "I mean, it's a good thing, right? It's what every Fae hopes for."

Captain unsteadily stands, then leans on her desk and stares beyond me into lost thoughts. Her silence is unsettling and I pinch the bridge of my nose. "I just thought we would've had more time, or maybe," I sigh and admit my selfish intent, Captain has never judged me, "I was hoping they would never cross paths. Even saying it aloud is awful, I have Orion, how could I wish that for the person I love?"

Captain's eyes dim finally, and she focuses on me with the same unreadable expression. "Are you sure? Tell me exactly what happened."

"I'm not an idiot Cap! I know what I saw, and so did Orion." I find myself standing over a rather calm Captain and take a shaky step back, knocking the chair with my leg. "Everyone did, the entire crew saw the way he was looking at her, and then they looked right at me, they *knew*. How could you not? The air was filled with their connection, I've read about such things but never saw it for myself, I didn't think it would be so palpable."

My heart beats wild with panic and my vision blurs, gut wrenching all the alcohol I've drank tonight. I hunch over and brace my hands on knees, cursing myself for falling so hard for him. I told myself I would drown in his love until this day came, but it's not enough. Captain's hands slide under my armpits and she takes the brunt of my weight, holding me in silence as the panic attack finishes consuming me.

"Have you given thought to the idea that Novak might not *want* to be with her? Not all mates are meant to be." Captain whispers and I stiffen.

"I can't hope for that, and I can't ask him to stay, it's not fair to him."

"But what about you, Alvis?" She whispers and I pull from her embrace gently, the tall Fae eye level with me. The last time someone asked me that, my entire life changed. Drunken footsteps clatter aboard the ship and my heart jumps at the thought of Novak not with them. Orion's presence steps onto the ship and I look over my shoulder at the closed door as if he's there.

"I don't want to know what happened, but is he ok?" I ask, but am answered by a very pissed off Novak throwing open the door. His icy flame filled eyes remind me of the day he killed Loyska, and they dart between Captain and I.

"What the fuck happened to you? I was fucking worried about you, I couldn't find you and no one knew where you went," Novak launches into a full lecture as he marches over to us with red cheeks and a mouthful of sass, standing on tip toes to berate me.

Captain clears her throat, arms crossed. "If you don't mind, I'd like to get some sleep. I have some business to attend to tomorrow." Novak's mouth hangs open and I resist the urge to brush away the hair covering his eyes. I may need to practice.

"You can't just leave me like that!" Novak yells, oblivious to Captain's flaring crimson eyes beside him.

"Will you fucking leave already? I need to sleep." Captain snarls and my heart races as I watch Novak's face crumple. I've never heard her talk to him this way. His surprise is brief, he takes my hand and drags me out without a word.

Disgruntled crew members lay passed out across the main deck, not able to make it to the crew's quarters below. I relish the feel of Novak's fingers around mine and for a moment it's like the tavern never happened, maybe Captain's right and I was worried over nothing. We pass through the blue fabric door of his room I allow myself a moment of hope. I won't say anything, this is his choice.

After we are in the safety of his always meticulously clean room, he finally turns to me with tears in his red rimmed eyes, and the shred of hope is stomped in with each drop that falls.

Fuck.

I cup his wet freckled cheeks with dark vined hands that encompass each side of his face, then kiss his forehead with trembling lips. "I have always meant what I said. I am always here for you, even if you are not mine." I murmur onto his warm skin and he clenches fistfuls of my cloak. Sobs rattle his body and he buries his face in my heated chest. I tuck him in tight to my body and pet his head.

"Yell at me, tell me I'm a selfish prick, kick my ass, say anything but that." He cries into my chest, but I can't do that. Despite how much my heart is breaking, I can't be angry with him right now.

"Shh, let's get you to bed."

In a swift movement I slide my arms under his legs and shoulders, then carry him to the still disheveled bed we made love in for hours during the early morning light when night twists with dawn. I tuck him in and pull the quilts his aunt made him around his neck, then kiss his forehead once more before leaving. "It's cold." He says with a shiver as I make it to the door, the two words break me. I clench the door frame with knuckles blanching, then step out without looking back.

I'm not surprised to find Orion waiting for me, knees tucked into his chest on the bed I haven't slept on in a year, since the first time Novak and I had sex together. For some reason his room always felt more like home to me than my own. I collapse onto the dusty bed and Orion stretches out so I can rest my head on his lap. The immense comfort I feel from reuniting with my twin after only hours of separation mixes with grief, another reminder of what Novak would've missed out on if I fought harder.

"You shouldn't have let him go." Orion remarks, staring at the only decorations in the dimly lit space, tapestries Novak collected for me from each town we've visited, their bright colors lining the walls. I flip onto my back and scowl at him, my head still in his lap.

"How can you say that? I've spent a lifetime keeping us from being separated. How can I do that to him?" I ask, flipping the pin on my cloak and hurriedly throwing the fabric off, though I'm still too hot.

"I can't explain it, but that female should not be mated to him." Orion whispers, fidgeting with my hair.

"Just stop, this isn't going to make me feel better." I say, sitting up as I wave him off.

"You think I would do that? I know you don't want my pity. Just let me show you." I stare at Orion, aghast why he's being so pushy about this. The female even resembles Novak in a way, her fair skin and blue eyes matching his.

131

"O, I couldn't stand to see them just *look* at each other, I don't want to see anything else." I bury my face in my hands and sigh, the image of the female's disgust at Novak's music coming to mind.

"Fine, you'll see tomorrow." Orion huffs, leaving the bed, and me.

"What?" I snap, head jolting up to stare at his figure paused at the tapestry door.

"Novak wants to show her the ship, before we leave." Orion informs me solemnly.

"We, as in all of us?" I ask, voice thin. Orion shakes his head, averting his eyes. "He already agreed, before talking to me?" I reaffirm, and Orion only nods. My ears ring and I stand, fists shaking as I attempt to comprehend. Disappointment and hurt are feelings I can handle, but he really agreed to leave the ship without talking to me at all, or Captain?

Those realizations only drive a fury laced spike of fire into my heart, and suddenly my entire body is trembling. Orion pushes his glasses up, finally meeting my wildly flashing violet eyes. "I'm telling you Alvis, something's not right. Trust me on this."

My mind races and I can only nod, then collapse onto the bed after Orion leaves me alone. Novak's scent is everywhere, though I can't tell if it's lingering in the musty room or if I'm going crazy. I stare up at the constellations I painted on the ceiling with Novak's direction, unable to fathom how my world has flipped so suddenly.

* * *

I didn't sleep.

The constellations on my ceiling are burned into my mind, my eyes burn and body is trapped by the bed. Orion prodded me through the bond at sunrise, but I didn't answer. It must be mid morning now, the ship is alive and Novak's cheerful voice perks my ears now and then. I don't think I can bear to say goodbye to him, or face his mate. Though I didn't hear her speak last night, the unfamiliar high pitched voice above alerts me to her presence.

I blink when Captain knocks on the door frame, her pointed boots visible opposite my purple tapestry. I sit up with a groan and rub my glass filled eyes. "Come in."

Captain casually approaches, then gestures to the mattress beside me. I nod and stretch my arms overhead, yawning wide. I arch a brow at the full ensemble she has on today, her white tunic laced with gold flows around her waist like a dress. The military style leather jacket, falchion at her side and glowing red eyes contrast her feminine interior.

"Well aren't you just dressed to impress?" I muse, pulling out the drawer in the stand beside my bed. I retrieve the pipe Novak had Lex make me a few months ago, the old Fae an artist in more ways than one. I caress the waves crashing down the length of the curving handle, smiling as I remember the day he gave it to me.

"Oh this? Tis' nothing." Captain says and I smirk, lighting fresh herbs packed loosely into the pipe. After a deep exhale releases a smoke ring, I pass the device to Captain. She partakes in a long drag and releases an airship composed of smoke that passes through my lingering smoke ring.

"Show off." I tease, leaning into Captain's side. We're the same height, but width wise she's half my size.

"I'll cut to the chase friend, if you don't want to say goodbye, you're not obligated to. I don't think I could, if I were you." Captain remarks bluntly and I glance sideways at her, taking the pipe back as I do. The voice trills again above, highly feminine and warmly welcomed by the Crew above. I swallow panic, anxiety and bile as I hear Novak holler in return.

"Have you talked to him yet?"

"*Ai*, early this morning before he went back to Okucha to fetch her."

"And he's really staying with her?"

"*Ai.*"

I I fill my lungs to the brim and give Captain the last turn, then hang my head and hide in my hands as the smoke releases. Captain's hand gently rests in between my flexed shoulder blades. "I know he loves you, and you him, so don't take this wrong way when you're obviously hurting, but I must say it to someone."

I lift my head from my hands and stare at her, finding uncharacteristic sadness leaking from her eyes. "We've grown up together, built this ship together. I asked him to stay, Al, and he told me no."

"Oh, Cap." I whisper, throwing my arms around her and holding her tight. Her body doesn't wrack with sobs, but she silently cries into my chest, muscles lax with grief.

I wish I could say it makes me feel better to see it's not just me Novak's leaving behind, but I've never seen Captain break before, and she's seen some of the most traumatic shit out of anyone I know. The idea of Novak being the cause of her grief breaks my brain.

"Only the Ancients know why our fates twine the way they do." I say half heartedly, resting my chin on her head.

"I was visited by an Ancient once." Captain admits, leaving my chest and wiping her eyes with her sleeve.

"When?" I ask quickly, eyes wide as Novak's music softly calls from above.

"Before I met Novak, the first time I visited the mainland. At first I thought she was just a Wild Fae, but then she gave me a prophecy, said I was the first to hear it." Captain sniffles, removing her hat to straighten the curved feather.

I take her and squeeze tight, causing the hat to fall to the floor. "The night," My words are halted by an invisible wall and I close my eyes, inhaling deep as I remember what Emeric told me. I still haven't shared my burdens with anyone other than Orion, though I still have nightmares about life in Silverbury.

"The night I met Novak, I tried to sink myself to the bottom of the lake."

"Why would you do such a thing?" Captain asks, taking my face in her searing hot hand. I flinch as she inhales deeply, resting both of her still sparking hands in her lap. "Sorry." She mutters and I wave her off.

"I was tired of all the blood on my hands, and Novak hated me so much. At that time, he was everything I never thought I'd be." I wipe my eyes, air flowing into my lungs easier than it did before. "An Ancient stopped me, or I stopped myself, I still don't know. Nothing she said make sense, but one part I've always believed was about Novak."

Captain's slender pointed ears lift, and she speaks the words on the tip of my tongue. "Walk with the poet who becomes a king, right?"

I nod, heart stopping for so long it causes Orion to tug on the bond and make sure I'm not dead. "My mother told me once poets are people who tell stories so vivid it's as if you're there, that's what his music feels like to me. I haven't told him though, I honestly thought it was all in my head."

"Was there anything else, with yours?" Captain asks, rising from the mattress and offering a hand as shouts emerge from the deck above. I check in with Orion, but when he doesn't answer I worry he's the culprit. I take her hand and tell Captain the rest, her brow furrows as she straightens her hat.

"I take it there was more to yours?" I ask and she shakes her head.

"We'll talk about it later, if you're going to say goodbye you better put something on that doesn't reek like alcohol." She says, glaring over her shoulder when she pauses at the door.

"I want to say goodbye. We live in Iverbourne, I could very well never see him again." I state, the thought straightening me.

"Will you ask him, if not for you, for me? Please?" Captain begs in a whisper barely stretching across the room, pricking the hairs along my arms and neck.

"I'll try, alright?" I say, stiffness and exhaustion plaguing my body. Captain nods with a sad smile. "Make sure he doesn't leave, kay?"

After she leaves I hurriedly yank open the drawer filled with my best clothes, the embroidered fabrics reserved for special occasions. I throw a combination of black trousers and a deep purple tunic detailed with silver thread on the mattress filled with crumpled blankets. Before dressing I wash my face with a wet cloth and comb through the tangled mess of coils upon my crown, then slip on the leather corded necklace I took off last night.

The simple cherry anchor is cracked in a few places now and beaten by every day wear, but when it rests on my sternum the familiar small weight comforts me. Novak made us a matching pair, showing me his the day after we buried Mother's ashes and performed the *levaya* at that pond. I don't intend to take the talisman off again until breaks, despite the impending outcome.

The crew eases into silence above, the gaggle of chatter and teasing among the lot fading into eerie quiet. Intense worry suddenly rushes over the bond from Orion and I dress in a hurry, then sprint into the sleeping quarters bare foot as I register what's happening. Captain shouts Novak's name with fury as I land on the deck above and face the ramp where the crew is gathered, blocking my view of the port.

"Wait!" I yell, shoving through the group with a heavy heart hammering out of my chest. First I see Captain standing on the edge of the ramp where it touches ground, encased in flames and fists shaking. I follow her stare and find Novak standing hand in hand with his mate a hundred feet away, backs turned to the ship. I know he must've heard me, but he doesn't turn.

I stand by Captain's side and cup my hands over my mouth. "You're really not going to say goodbye?" I shout with all my might, startling Captain. Novak flinches and glances over his shoulder at me, sapphires flash with sadness when they catch with mine. The female at his side glares at me, then gently cups his cheek and directs his gaze forward. Captain snarls as the pair disappear into thin air, traveling to who knows where.

Tears unabashedly stream down my face and I drop my eyes to my bare feet glued to the ramp. Captain rests a hand on my right shoulder, and Orion does the same on my left. I shrug them both off and tighten my fists, short nails cutting into my palms. "What the hell, Cap?" I ask, voice choked with fury.

"Before I came up, Orion got into it with Novak because that *tannin* was whining for him to quit playing, apparently she was in a hurry to get out of here." I glare sideways at Orion but he only stares with a hard glare at the place where Novak once stood, eyes flashing between lilac and white. Captain turns and faces me, flames extinguished.

"I asked him to wait for you, which ticked her off more. The last straw was when he introduced me as Captain and Sage thought he was making fun of her by not telling my real name."

"I can't believe this fucking shit, that's not Novak!" I snap, finally losing my composure. Captain leaves me and Orion with a fresh gleam of Aether in her hard set eyes, shouting orders to the crew to begin lift off. "Can I see?" I ask, but Orion rests a hand on my shoulder and shakes his head.

"Come on, let's get to work." He mutters, surprising me with such few words. I don't shrug his hand off, I can't move at all. "Does it make a difference seeing how awful it was? He made his choice and we still have a promise to Captain."

"You're right." I sigh, raking a hand through my coils before pressing my forehead to his. I follow his leave onto the ship, then run the crank and pull the ramp up. Aether engines roar to life and the familiar vibration hums the decking below me once more. I am soon lost in the chaos unfolding around me, utterly useless.

Somehow I find myself seated on the floor of the helm, hiding behind Captain as she navigates us to our next adventure. I nurse the pipe with waves crashing along it's grain whilst clutching the anchor on my neck, eyes closed and chest heavy. I imagine the strong wind rushing my cheeks is the same winter air I experienced with Novak and the fireflies, and somehow I have no more tears to shed in that moment.

Letters from Home.

Beakglen, The Townhouse
A Few Weeks after 'The Incident'

"Hey, wake up."

I groan and throw myself over in bed, further securing darkness with blankets around my head. Umber shoves my shoulder once more and I moan, a soul twisting hangover coursing through my body. "Why are you so bossy? This is supposed to be a vacation."

"Vacation or not, I think two in the afternoon is an appropriate time to get up for the day." She drawls, heavy footsteps fading across my bedroom in the town home. What used to be Novak's room, but he doesn't need it anymore.

"Who cares." I pull down just enough of the blanket to spy the Fae with springy oceanic hair shiny and clean, unlike mine. She waits patiently at the door and I sit up in a huff. "Happy now? Take it you're my babysitter then? Where's O?"

"I'm not *anyone's* babysitter, and where do you think Orion is?" Umber warns, silver eyes flashing with annoyance. She's dressed in typical *Yule* season fashion, a grey woolen sweater and thick trousers, covered by a black cloak as the Fae is always cold, even inside. I furrow my brows, contemplating what day it is. Wait, is today Yule?

"To answer your question, no, it's tomorrow. I do have an unfortunate gift for you, and I've been debating on whether to give it to you or not." She murmurs, retrieving a letter from an inner pocket of her cloak.

"What are you, a mind reader?" I swing my legs over the side of the bed swiftly, inviting dizziness to steal my vision temporarily. She bites her cheek and strides over, thrusting a small envelope towards me.

"I received this yesterday, and I feel like you're the one who should write him back."

"Hmm?" I take the worn envelope and flip it over, finding Umber's name written in Novak's near unintelligible writing. I swallow fear and stare at her, jaw tightening as I do.

"Just read it, I already have and am going to throw it away if you give it back." Umber says, waving me off as she opens the door. I study the envelope and she glances over her shoulder, then clears her throat. "Captain will be staying tonight, so I suggest you lay off the alcohol, or disappear if you can't."

I nod to her in silence and the moment she shuts the door, I open the envelope.

Umber,

I know you've never liked me much, so I suppose that's why it's easier to tell you this than the others. I imagine Captain has nothing but disappointment for me now and as always, she was right to be pissed at me. I hope you get this before Yule so you can tell her and the others l'shanah tovah tikatevu for me, though I doubt anyone wants to hear what I have to say, and I can't blame them.

I've been staying in Vabel, there's snow and it's quite cold here, but Maverick's place has a huge hearth that keeps me warm enough. Who is Maverick, you ask? Well, he's my long lost friend I've thought dead for years, turns out he escaped from the massacre his brother died in. Not only that, but he's Sage's husband.

Yup, my mate is married to the man I've thought dead for years.

You don't know how long it took me to write this far and admit that fact, the past few days have been surreal enough as it is. It started when Sage admitted she didn't actually live in Okucha, she lives here, in Vabel. Before we walked in the door of this huge mansion, she says to me, "Oh, this cannot go on any longer, you remember Maverick, right? We're married."

Ai, I know it sounds dramatic, but it really was like that. I have no idea why she brought me here, though she told Maverick she found me for him, apparently he talks about me quite often to her and she recognized me right off. That's why she stared at me in the bar, not because of the bond.

I know she can feel it, it's so bizarre to have this connection to someone else and you think they feel it too, but really you're just an idiot. Enough of the bullshit, you've probably stopped reading this by now, I'm become so boring. Maverick treats me well enough, he's one of the few humans who decided to brave Vabel once more and all the people here really look up to him, he even gave me a studio to teach music and stay in.

I can stay as long as I like, but I have to admit, I really miss home.

The Akar

I jump upwards and throw myself across the room, landing in a hurry at the study desk covered in alcohol stains, weapons and drunken vent sketches leaking with anger infused ink. I sweep it all off the desk onto the ground, the crashing of blades and empty glass bottles fold down my charcoal fluffed ears down. I yank out various drawers of the roll top desk, great craftsmanship ruined by my carelessness. Parchment finally reaches my hurried fingers in the bottom drawer and I begin scrawling nonsense in moments.

~~Nova,~~

~~Novak,~~
~~If you miss home so much why don't you come home?~~

~~Novak,~~
~~The ship has been lonely without you~~

~~Novak,~~
~~All is forgiven, just come home.~~

~~Novak,~~
~~I can't stop thinking about you and I don't care if you can't love me.~~

Novak,

I've been thinking about you and hope this letter finds you before tomorrow's moon, I will send as much Aether as I can so it finds you in time.

If you're thinking about coming home, we all miss you, and I think you should. Captain has been especially grumpy and Orion needs someone to knock him down a few pegs in that chess game of yours, I'm no match for him.

I'm not asking you to come home just for me, I want you to be happy, with your family that truly loves you.

L'shanah tovah tikatevu, my dear friend. I'll be at our place tomorrow night, if you decide you want some company on the holiday.

The Dumb One

I wait for the ink to dry and read his letter once more, heart thundering as my fingers caress the last line of his messy writing. I bite my cheek and fold my letter carefully, tucking it into a simple envelope. On the front I scrawl *Zemer* with care, then seal the back with wax using the small seal of a faerie skull and crossbones, the seal of Captain.

Before sending the letter off, I retrieve the small pouch I had with me on the night I lost Novak, taking it out from a small hidden compartment in the desk. Shaking fingers retrieve the ring inside and I study the plain wooden circlet in my palm. I broke eight of them before I could make one come out right and I couldn't manage any fancy designs like Novak can, but I was so proud of it. Lexeran helped me, before he and Captain's friendship went south.

I put the ring back inside the pouch, then tuck it away into the compartment. I shut part of my heart away, allowing myself some hope as I hold the envelope in my outstretched palms. I close my eyes and Aether bubbles to the surface of my skin as I focus on Novak's familiar scent lingering from his letter on the desk. In the forefront of my mind is the town I once burned to the ground. Vabel.

An icy draft swirls over my fingers and my breath hitches, focus nearly breaking as Aether splits time and space. The physical fabric of my world tears over my fingertips, ripping through the seam just enough to take my desperate words to Novak across hundreds of snow filled miles. I send every bit of my magic with the envelope to ensure it finds him, and brings him home.

* * *

The Next Day

Gold and silver streaks across the sky, a plentiful meteor shower blesses the twin moons bathing in the late night air of *Yule*, the shortest day of the year. The third and last night of celebrations echoes through the snow filled Glen in the distance, the village celebrating the spoils of the Great Hunt. The moons are at their peak, which brings them so close to this painful world. The fireflies were waiting me when I arrived at dusk, a flock twice the size of the group I watched with Novak have distracted me for hours.

"It's been awhile Mother, sorry I don't have anything to bring you today." I murmur, hands fidgeting as I stare at the spot opposite the pond Novak and I buried the jar, underneath a golden birch sapling. Loneliness rides with the gusts of wind blowing my cloak hood back, I haven't felt this way since the night I met him.

Knees connect with frozen mud and I bury my face in scarred hands bound by hideous bonds imitating beautiful nature. Hot tears contrast with the below freezing atmosphere, and my feet ache terribly. Crimson from the great boar's life stains my hands, my victory from this morning. The luminescent turquoise pond before me is almost as bright as the celestial bodies in the sky and the galaxies they outshine, so much beauty surrounds me here in this hidden treasure.

Though hours must pass before I face the dawn, the stars have already begun writing the days of the new year, and my heart has nothing but pain inside it.

I truly thought he would come.

Rivers of blood entangle with orange flames on the horizon, lined with the darkest clouds of fleeting night. Twigs snap and I exhale, then erupt from the thicket and embrace the wild beast, my blade meets the thick hide protecting it's throat in an instant. The boar thrashes and I keep it pinned under me, the creature's razor like tusks tear apart my forearms as it bleeds out, fighting until the very last moment.

Pain is a welcome feeling, as the boar's spirit relents and leaves this world in reluctant peace, I utter a prayer.

"Your flesh shall feed the hungry, your hide shall protect an hearth, your tusks shall forge weapons, and nothing shall be wasted from your sacrifice. Your spirit, may it find peace, and favor with the Ancients. On this Great Hunt I ask only one request, and that is to bring my lover home."

144

* * *

"Hey, what're you doing out here?" Captain's voice pulls me from a frozen slumber and I groggily open my eyes, lashes breaking apart. I fell asleep in the snow beside the pond and every bone is stiff, Captain's feathered hat is all I can make out against the first rays of morning. Gentle warmth meets my cheeks after she sits me up, slowly bringing me back to life so I don't go into shock.

"Mm, my toes." I say, groaning. "I might have a problem there." I straighten my leg with shaking gloved hands, my boots had dipped into the slick ice mixed with slush at the shoreline. I flinch as painful tingles fill my cheeks and I wave Captain off, her hands hovering over my face.

"Fuck off, you're half frozen, you know what state your brother is in because of you?"

"Ugh, don't pull that card, it's not like I meant to fall asleep out here, did you see that size of that boar?" I tease, cracked lips upturning. Captain rolls her flaring orange eyes, veiling a smile.

"Tasted better than it looked." She shrugs and I chuckle, warmth slowly returning to my extremities as her bare fingers hover my arms, then my legs. "You were waiting for him, weren't you?" Captain asks, keeping her focus on her softly glowing bare hands.

"I'm always waiting for him."

Sanity or Blood?

Arca Hallow Airspace, Sylvan Court
Two Days Later

"Just for the record, I think this is a bad idea." I mumble, leaning over the port side railing at the helm. Captain scoffs at me, raven hair filled with snow and the feathers on her hat are iced over. Her eyes aren't the only ones glowing today, the weather has finally broken through that stubborn head of hers, convincing her to let Orion and I help power the engines. Orion shivers beside Captain, glaring sideways at me.

"How is delivering presents a bad idea? I'm not about to break tradition now, if he isn't going to come to me, then I'll go to him." Captain muses, her voice full of dark humor and trouble. I straighten and pull the black hood of my cloak up as the lights of Arca Hallow glimmer beneath us through the early morning hour. Vabel is quite small and doesn't have an airport, so Arca Hallow is the closest we're going to get, though it's hundreds of miles away and we can't freely dock like we do in Glen.

"I still can't believe you're going to leave the ship. Have you even touched grass in the last few years, besides at home?" Orion teases, attempting to lighten the mood as he tightens his own cloak around himself. I figure we have two, maybe three hours before daylight hits.

"Oh come now, it hasn't been *that* long." She waves him off as she turns down engines. "Get to work, we'll be leaving before first light so no partying tonight." Captain pointedly glares at me and I narrow my brows, leaving with Orion in defeated silence to organize the landing crew. I can't argue too much.

When no one could find me the day after *Yule* and Orion was chilled to the bone, I nearly died all over again when Captain announced we would be paying Novak a visit. I glance at Umber working in the rigging above, she insists she didn't tell Captain about the letter, but she must've for Captain to act like this.

"You are such an idiot sometimes." Orion chides from beside me at the stern, both of us supervising the crew tossing ropes and fastening the sails as the ship touches down in the docking station. There are only three stations here and the other two are empty which brings me relief, Sylvan lands are the last place I want to be. The draw on Orion and I's Aether dissipates and our glowing violet eyes dim, no longer tangling with the numerous lanterns lining the ship.

"I know that, but elaborate?"

"She's doing this because you almost died hoping that idiot would show up, and if that's not enough, it's pretty obvious she misses him. Shouldn't you be happy about this?" Orion asks, glancing at me sideways as eerie silence thickens between us.

"I told him to come home and he didn't, he's made his choice. It's time to stop bothering him." I decide and walk away from Orion, hairs standing up on my neck as we leave the raised stern and step onto the main deck. The port is eerily quiet, usually there is a master that greets incoming ships and collects the toll, plus compensation for keeping their mouth shut.

Captain is still at the helm, scanning over the murmuring crew who have suddenly paused their duties. "What's going on?" I ask Hugo, standing beside the horned Fae at the back of the crowd. The small grey eyed Fae blinks, gaze unwavering as he lifts a finger to the horizon in the east, beyond the folded down ramp. I follow his shaky point, breath leaving as I see what he does.

Despite the distance and abysmal night hiding the moons, the terrifying sight is crystal clear. Gigantic thick abysmal clouds of smoke mushroom into the sky, fire licking the thick cover of clouds. Thunderous explosions crack the air overhead and the ship rocks on the scaffolding. Shouts and dizzying voices follow as waves of aftershocks rumble through the ground.

"By the Ancients, what is that?" Orion breathes shakily beside me, his hand resting on my left shoulder. I shoot a look up to Captain who is staring at the clouds, feet glued to the helm and mouth wide open.

"Captain! We need to go." I shout, my feet taking control and hauling me in the direction of the silent airport. Four strides. Horses, we need horses.

Five strides. Wait, weapons, I need weapons.

I skid to a halt in the dirt and as I turn around, an Aether hole drops two figures onto the ground before me. Screams and chaos erupts from the ship and Captain shoves the crew out of her way, but I already have Sage by the shoulders.

"Where is he?" I growl, Aether humming through every inch of my being. Orion kneels by the unconscious man in Sage's arms and Captain stands behind me, both silent as they await her answer. The arrogant beauty stares into my eyes, and I swear no remorse floats in them as she stares me down.

"You need to hurry." Her fierceness is replaced by a facade of fright and Captain's shoulders alight with soft orange flames, but she remains calm as she kneels beside me. Now isn't the time to bicker.

"What are we walking into?" Captain asks, pointing to the growing plumes of smoke and fire in the distance.

"I, I don't know, we were leaving the tavern together and some mercenaries found us, well we thought they were, but Novak recognized them as something odd, oh what did he call them... *Nafshyi?*" Sage stutters and I shoot upwards, trembling as I pace frantically.

"How many? Where?" I ask.

"A doz, dozen, in Vabel. There was none of *that* when we left, but then again I couldn't travel here until the last twenty miles." Sage gestures to the hellfire, filth lining her torn clothes. She does look like she's been through something, I really don't trust her but at the same time, if what she says is true ...

A dozen.

"Brother, Novak can stand his own, let's find horses." Orion orders, halting my pacing as he steadies me by my shoulders, staring me directly in the eyes.

"We don't have time!" I shout and thrust a hand to a new explosion of smoke and fire erupting in the distance, another quake nearly taking me off my feet.

Captain approaches swiftly and extends an open hand to me. "Quick, we can't stay here anyway. I won't be able to land but I can get you close enough to travel down." I take her hand and nod, then we sprint towards the ship. Surprise, guilt and relief twist through me at the empty dirt where Sage and the unconscious Maverick were. Anger fills me that she is abandoning her mate, but relief washes over the fury for the same reason.

"We're gonna have to work together to get this old beast in the air again, I know you're all tired, but Novak needs our help." Captain hollers as she crosses the main deck and the crew wastes no time, Aether alighting every pair of Fae eyes. Sails flare as the ship hums with an intensity I've never heard before.

Every crew member here loves Novak, and it only took the words 'he needs our help' to set every pair of feet into motion, like we just didn't fly for over twelve hours. I duck into the crew's quarters below and enter my room without hesitation, finding additional blades and the heaviest pair of fighting leathers I own.

A soft knock on the door frame perks my ears and I finish dressing. "Come in."

Umber walks through the door, shaking out her freshly trimmed coils standing inches above her crown. She crosses her thick arms, broad shoulder muscles flexing under her leather jacket as I stand across from her. "Alvis, I hate to always be the bearer of bad news, but I won't baby you like the others do. Have you given credence to thought Novak may already be dead?"

My scarred hands tighten into fists, resisting the urge to encapsulate her throat. A deep growl emits from my chest as my jaw tightens and I take a step backwards from the person who has been a sharp rock for me to hold onto in these last few months. I wish I could say I'm the type of male who could grief in abstinence, but the only time I don't think about Novak is when I'm with Umber, and that's only because of the solid fact she's nothing like him.

I don't love Umber, not in the romantic way. Her and I are both without who we truly want, and we fill the space emptiness leaves behind. She has never referred to the Fae by name, but the longing in her eyes is unmistakable when she's slipped up recounting memories in bed, the most at ease Umber ever is.

"He's not dead." I state, like a child.

"Don't tell me your heart is telling you he is, or some gushy crap like that. Be realistic, in the ten minutes you've been down here the atmosphere has filled with smoke, come look." I step outside of my room, Umber trailing behind with a heavy step. Smoke wafts through the crew's quarters, rivers of charcoal scented smoke weaving around the wooden rungs worn by boots over decades.

"Are they taken care of?" I point to the room the healers share, worry creasing my brow as I search the quarters for anyone sleeping in the smoke. I've learned three out of the four female healers residing on the ship are mute, a custom Typhan enacted to mark a troublesome slave. The healers prefer solitude and I do my best to respectfully avoid them, as does Orion.

"*Ai*, they're in Captain's quarters with Vesper, as are the others who can't tolerate the air so well. Everyone's ready and taken care of, don't worry." Umber assures me and I nod, only then do we climb up the ladder through thick smoke.

I jump onto the main deck and instinctively look for Orion, though I feel his presence safe at Captain's side at the helm well before I see him. A cacophony of colors fill the deck as Fae eyes pierce the night thick with murmured fear and smoke. Umber and I arrive at the helm, and she truly wasn't kidding.

The brig is bathed with black smoke so thick, visibility is near impossible as the foul smelling smog intertwines with the moonless night. Captain steers us in silence towards our explosive reality, our brows furrowed with extreme concentration. I swallow the lump of fear building in my throat as I behold the distant fishing village tucked at the bottom of a small mountain.

Beyond the prow, flames encapsulate the entire horizon. Hues of flaring crimson and jet black compose towers of smoke and fire that scrape the sky. I stagger and Orion is there to steady me, an arm around my shoulder as the ship speeds towards the village, but not fast enough. He and I aren't powering the ship but magic is primed in my veins, though drained from our already arduous trip to the port. Umber stands at my other side, the three of us waiting beside Captain who sheds silent tears.

As I stand there filled with dread, I realize how I know Nova is still alive. Tears will not fall, and they would if the *Zemer* were truly dead.

The world itself would mourn the death of him, the poet who is to become a king.

* * *

Novak

Pain has never frightened me, a fleeting sensation that only proves the fact you're still alive. So long as there is pain, there is life. I believe there is a saying similar to this belief. As above, so below, and I feel this applies here.

I had fought with every inch of my soul, managing to down three of the brain washed bastards before they finally pinned me down. I can do nothing as a surgical like blade is procured in the largest of the *Nafshyi's* hands, the leader stands before my kneeling body held in place by his men. One has a fistful of my hair, tilting my head back so the blood flowing from my nose trickles down my throat. Each of my arms are restrained by two males, and my Aether is drained.

"Yes, quite excessive, but your spirit is still fighting, hence the overkill." The leader smirks, delighting in my release of emotion, surprise. "Yes, I can hear every word bouncing in that head of yours. Doesn't it ever get tiring? Talking so much?"

"You'd be surprised how many times this mouth got me out of trouble." I chuckle, spitting out blood as it overflows my mouth from where I was knocked sideways by an orb of magic.

The remaining five Nafshyi stand behind their leader, smirking at my figure restrained by their comrades. Only two females compose the group, though I know better than anyone the females that survive the Aether infusions are much stronger than their male counterparts. I grimace internally remembering how much magic it took to kill Loyska, and the thought darkens the leader's face which lowers to mine. His knees drop inches from my own in the dirt.

The village is silent around us, the once small Vabel is now a thriving town filled with life, the head start Captain and I gave this place plummeting it into harmony. "Well, that confirms it." His charcoal tufted ears flick, one violet and one silver eye flashing so bright I'm temporarily blinded. Fingers brush my right ear, then harshly grab the tip, pulling outwards. I jerk backwards but the hand fisted in my hair tightens.

"I heard a human loving brat killed my dear Loyska, and you've confessed your sin right to your executioner."

My vision returns as his fatal words finish, and a devilish smile fills his thin face as the surgical blade glints in the moonlight once more. I spit in his face and smile, just so I can say I have a shred of pride in my last few moments. Without wiping the saliva off his skeletal face the leader smiles, and I close my eyes. Dignity is swiped away, heart wrenching as the blade cleanly slices through the cartilage and fur of my ear.

Warmth drips onto my bare shoulder, searing pain ruminating from under the meticulous work of the *Nafshyi*. I submit, not allowing one moan or cry to escape, nor a change of expression. I repeat the words I've agonized over for days, thinking only of his face. The anchor once around my neck was split apart when they finally got their hands on me, and it's carcass is somewhere in the street with the rest of my fight.

"I just you want to be happy."

The only person who has truly made me happy I hurt beyond belief, and as another wave of pain rolls from my other ear, I curse myself for throwing away what we had. I should've gone to him. Hell, I should've never left.

"Hmm, this isn't good enough." A dissatisfied growl rumbles from above and I open my eyes, hot stickiness flowing down my cheeks. Blood trickles down my chest and I smile wide, which earns a slap to the side of the head, directly on a freshly rounded ear. I finally break, a shout cracking my chest.

"I have an even better idea." A high pitched voice splits the air and as the tight hand in my hair straightens me to face forward again, fear settles in my chest as I watch one of the females whisper into her superior's ear. A devious grin contagiously spreads across the group, they must be silently communicating.

"Tell me brat, have you heard of the *l'aryik* ritual?"

I stiffen, ears ringing as the sleeping world continues beyond this back alley filled with fear and evil. The leader laughs, my subtle body movement betrays me as my eyes turn stone cold. "There hasn't been a soul alive who can perform that and not become empty themselves."

"And *we're* not supposed to be alive, and yet here we are." The choppy black haired female at the leader's side snaps, her kaleidoscope eyes filled with a dizzying array of colors. "Your boy toy started this carousel ride of things that shouldn't exist, it's only fair you join the list."

"I have no connections, do what you will." I dare, staring the female in her eyes with a raised chin. She looks up to the leader with a gleam in her eye and he passes her the bloodied blade, earning a bright smile from the child like female. She strides to me within seconds, the back of her hand smacks across my cheek in a swift movement.

"Don't. Lie." She orders, lifting my chin and squeezing tight. My brows furrow and I stare up at her. "Daddy dearest has been watching his favorite son for quite some time, and we all know what you mean to him."

I lock eyes with the satisfied leader off to the side, fear finally taking place in my soul. That's why-

"Why I can't hurt him? Oh, don't worry, if this doesn't kill you, you will wish you were by the time she's done with you. Typhan doesn't need you, just for sonny boy to come running when his puppy cries."

"It would appear you've miscalculated, as I said, I have no connections,

I used to, but no longer." Relief fills me for the first time since I left, they would've hurt him using me.

"Oh? Is that why we heard a certain ship with gold sails was head to Arca Glen? The only airport nearby? Couldn't be you had visitors coming?" The leader takes a flask from his comrade as the wild female before me brings the blade to rest at my collar bone, waiting for the final command. I struggle under the hands holding me in place and snarl, the entire situation having flipped on it's head.

Stubborn fucking bastard, I didn't answer his letter so I bet he's on his way to give me an earful, and I won't be around to hear it. By the time they find out, these *Nafshyi* will have killed me.

"Try to survive the ritual then, so you can watch the blood bath when they get here." The leader raises his drink to me, then slugs it back as the blade penetrates inches the skin above my collarbone. I writhe and cry out, as the knife begins carving further down my chest it takes more hands to hold me still. The ritual is dark magic, unused since the Golden age and rumored to take away a Fae's Aether.

Hours pass before consciousness finally offers to leave, though my body went slack after the first hour of runes being meticulously carved inches deep into my torso. Overlapping blood filled valleys lines my sides, and belly is next before I'm rolled over so the knife can finish bloodletting my back and withdrawing the weak magic left in my deflated veins.

Dirt mingles with the injuries lining every inch of my front and as the blade meets the back of my neck, I can no longer hold on to the fantasy I've held tight to through the hellish torture. Though he would really have no way of knowing where I am, or even making it here in time, I have held onto the image of Alvis appearing in this evil filled alley way and saving me.

But how could he or the others even stand a chance against these beasts when I couldn't?

As I fade out of the world and into a comforting cool sea, I digest the last conversation I hear. "I think he's dead, should I keep going?"

"Don't stop until he's covered in the *tannin's* mark, even in death he could be dangerous. I'm honestly surprised it was that easy."

Disappointment follows my soul down into the velvety ocean surrounding my tired spirit, and I fight against the soft tug pulling me downwards.

"Why are you still fighting?" A deep voice intones around me, vibrating my ghostly form. Though I cannot see or *feel* having a body, I can imagine the pout I must be putting on, like I did when Twila said I couldn't I be a hero, because I'm too mischievous.

"It shouldn't be *easy* to kill me. I've gone through too much for it to be easy." I argue and the tug momentarily lessens, leaving me free floating in the empty darkness.

A soft laughter vibrates the molecules around me. "You have not stopped fighting since day one, if I remember correctly, dear wanderer."

The words have me eagerly at attention, though I know better than to interrupt whatever being I have the audience of.

"I shall give you a choice. You can have passage to what awaits you beyond this place, or you can return, though I will warn you. You will have an incredibly difficult road ahead, filled with sacrifice, you will lose the ones you love and suffer great pain before you find happiness."

I contemplate my choices for what seems like an eternity, but time has no meaning here. "I *will* find happiness, for more than a fleeting moment, before the next time I meet you?"

"You will find happiness, and leave a mark greater on this world than anyone before you, but do not forget, it will be with great cost."

"Sanity, or blood?" I ask, and that question seems to delight the being.

"Both."

Never Falter.

___

Alvis

We hover inside a soot cloud, nothing visible through the crackling atmosphere, the coordinates of Vabel supposedly under the ship. I swallow audibly and look over the railing with Captain, Orion, and every other terrified crew member. Nothing but the sound of crackling fires hidden by layers of smoke meet our ears, from this low altitude we should be able to at least hear people screaming.

"Can you even travel down there without having a clear view of where to put your feet?" Umber mutters from my right and I glance to her, then to my brother who is shaking at my left. I pat my chest and make sure the flask from Captain is secure, our only way out of there in a hurry.

"We have to try." I say, heart thundering out of my chest.

"Still think he's alive?" Umber asks, temporarily drawing my attention, and Captain's.

"We will be waiting a few miles to the south, the wind is blowing towards the mountains but I don't want to be close in case it changes." Captain reiterates the plan and I nod, it's too risky for more than just

Orion and I to go, she needs all the Aether she can get to keep the ship in the air.

"I don't doubt your traveling skills, but take this so it's easier to find us." Umber murmurs, placing a raw malachite stone in my hand. Even as a Prince of the most profitable gemstone supplier of Iverbourne, I've never seen a malachite in person. I press my forehead to Umber's, then kiss her cheek.

"Thank you." I say, and she nods, joining Captain's side.

"Bring him back." Captain orders, and I smile bitterly. I take Orion's hand in silence and squeeze tight, our fluorescent purple eyes locked on the other.

"You ready?" Orion asks, his voice trembling in my mind.

"Let's find our first mate."

With a solid snap cracking through the air, time and space is split apart once more as Orion and I travel through molecules bending to our will. I focus on the image of the town square I once burned to pieces myself, and in seconds we land before a massive building engulfed in flames.

Fire consumes the village around us, half charred animals, Fae and humans lay everywhere in the street, trapped by flames infused with Aether. The flickering plumes of heat scatter and jump, behaving in a way that almost seems life like. Orion draws a translucent shield around us as I begin to cough, our bodies immediately covered by a rust colored soot.

"We don't have much time." Orion barks and I spin in place, nothing looks familiar or remotely like a village anymore. A dystopian land filled with dead bodies, scattered among the charcoaled remains of buildings. A flicker of movement draws my attention to the west side of the square, and Orion follows my stare as we both ready our weapons, my sword and the staff Emeric gifted Orion not long ago. Another shadow has me turning on my heel once more, a presence toying with my peripherals.

I press my back to Orion's, an icy presence raises my hackles and I track the shadowed figure as it approaches me, darting through fire. A loose humanoid body clouded by shimmering darkness slips out of an alley collapsing inward, it's form travels through rubble like a wisp. I raise my sword out of habit, even though it's obvious nothing physical will keep this thing at bay. Orion grips my shoulder, eyes wide and staff lowering. I stare at him incredulously, but when he nods at the figure and I follow his terrified gaze, my heart drops.

Twin pools of crimson evil await in the shadow's face, cloudiness settles to reveal a familiar slender body, although his skin is entirely ethereal and filled with galaxies, complexion reminiscent of galaxies. A fine tailored suit of black and grey smoke dresses the being as he rolls his neck. Deep laughter rolls from the demon, the sound grates my ears as if mountains are crashing together. When his joy ends, beautiful wings composed of charcoal feathers and shadows release from his back, the wingspan stretching over thirty feet.

Flames around us shoot into the air with a renewed vigor, heat and smoke clamping down on Orion's fading shield. As I think about raising a shield to assist, Orion shakes his head. "Save it, I have a feeling you're gonna be on the defense in other ways."

The being tilts it's head as it takes casual steps towards us. I straighten my spine and hold my ground, as does Orion. "I was planning on killing you immediately, but it seems this spirit is quite attached to yours. Listening to the idiot beg while I kill you slowly will be much more satisfying."

Warmth flows from my ears and I wonder if it's blood from the torturous voice rattling my ear drums. I drop my sword as Aether surges through my veins, electrifying my palms with vigor as I prepare for battle. "Speak plainly, and I may spare you your life." I order, stepping out of Orion's protective shield, despite his silent protests.

Violet flames crawl from my hands to my shoulders, contrasting against the crackling red dystopia around us. The shadow takes a step closer until we are face to face and the realization slams into me like a ton of bricks. Claws longer than my arm reach around my Aether protected neck, my magic singes the beast and brings surprise to it's face.

Surprise is replaced by dark laughter as the being claps it's talons together, a shock wave emanating from the motion which nearly knocks me backwards. "No wonder he is so drawn to you, your magic is exquisite, the mutilated magic from those pests doesn't hold a candle to yours, I can't even touch you. Why is that?"

"What have you done to Novak?" I shout into the small distance between us, lifting a palm filled with a fluorescent orb of lilac, the sphere growing with every second. A hint of anxiety washes over the being's face and I take a step closer, which results in him taking a step back. This beast is afraid of me?

"Don't get cocky." Orion warns, grounding me like he always does. I need both hands now to handle the sphere, the orb filling with every bit of Aether I have left.

"His body is now mine, and soon his spirit will be replaced by all the darkness in the world, broken like all those before him."

"You must not know who you're fucking with, because the *Zemer* never stops fighting."

The demon and I hurl our attacks in synchronicity and I am ill prepared for the impact, underestimating my power and the beast's onslaught. Orion is ready, his arms and shield envelope me as a jagged tendril of night rips across the space and intercepts my explosive orb of Aether. He and I both fall, shadows lazily compress Orion's flickering shield and I cough up blood, aftershocks of weak magic convulse through my body.

Orion groans, struggling on his knees with hands overhead, the white vines along his body glowing bright. I roll onto my side with great difficulty so I don't choke, vision gone as I fade in and out of nauseating consciousness. Through Orion's eyes I see the beast standing just outside the translucent shield, much more familiar than he was before. No longer clouded in shadows and ethereal skin is restored to freckles, Novak's body is still not his own, once glowing red eyes are now completely black and devoid of pupil.

"I have an idea, but I need-" Before Orion can finish shouting the request aloud I transfer the rest of my energy and inklings of Aether to him through our bond, and immediately pass out.

* * *

Orion

Shit. Shit. Shit.

The shield ricochets forward and my hands shake in the air as I struggle to control it. Alvis' sudden boost of Aether transforms weak lilac magic to a fluorescent purple. I shove back heavy darkness filled with malice as the reinvigorated shield slowly ensnares the surprised writhing beast before me. My heels dig into the charred soil as it screams, though it's voice is now twisted with something Fae. Novak.

I thought it was just Alvis' Aether the beast can't touch, but the closer my shield presses in on the wild being, the more it screams into the earth, body steaming as my magic presses into it's skin. Alvis' shallow breaths at my feet focus me and I slowly lift the shield, just enough so it's no longer touching Novak's body.

I take a wavering step forward, then two, mind spinning as blood drains from my nose. I stand over the dome and stare down into twin pits of darkness, their focus on the night sky above. I drop to my knees at the edge of the shield which slowly draws the attention of the beast.

Blood seeps from his tear ducts and nose, dribbling from the corners of his cracked lips. Even from his ears, and I realize something has happened to them, but I cannot tell what exactly from under all the dried and fresh blood.

Such a chilling vision of Novak's face possessed with unfamiliar eyes, damaged by me, is one I will never get out of my head. A dark chuckle emits from him along with a bloodthirsty grin, and my brows narrow together in confusion. "You can have him back, for now. I look forward to playing with you again." He winks at me, then shudders, a flash of sapphire replaces black before Novak's body goes slack.

I withdraw my shield at once, too fast as the energy rebounds in my body, dizzying me further for a moment. When I regain my senses I crawl over to Novak and press my ear to his bare chest, finding a thready heartbeat under a criss-cross of lacerations filling his torso. Flames encapsulate every way out, heat blistering my skin and Novak's.

Panic fuels me as I look back and see fire creeping on Alvis' unmoving figure. I slide my hands under Novak's legs and shoulders, groaning as I struggle to stand under my own weight, let alone his as well. "Fuck!" I shout, voice cracking as I cough on smoke, adrenaline tampered by exhaustion.

"Never falter, child." Mother's voice drifts around me, whether it's in my head or she's speaking to me through the wind, it empowers me all the same. I straighten with Novak's dead weight in my arms and make it to Alvis with wavering steps, collapsing as I drop Novak onto his unconscious body. I shakily reach into Alvis' leather vest and find the malachite, then the flask.

The quartz container is simmering and I hurriedly unscrew the cap, then inhale pressurized Aether. I clench the stone in my fist so tight it draws blood, then hover my hand over my brother and friend so sticky crimson drops onto their burning bodies. I close my eyes and wrap my arms around both of them, then focus every bit of borrowed Aether and willpower I have to travel the three of us to the ship, hopefully in one piece

The Banishing.

Captain

"We should've gone together, splitting up is always the worst idea." I mutter, pacing the helm. Umber stands at attention by the steering wheel, watching the crew wait impatiently below. All of us have had our eyes on the unending fire and smoke rolling from where we left the twins, but when those flames shot into the sky minutes ago, I wasn't able to watch any longer.

"We cannot risk everyone else to go to them, you know that."

"I didn't suggest we do so!" I shout, stalling my step to stare at the rugged female.

"You didn't have to, I know you've been thinking it ever since we left." Umber quips and I take off my hat, then throw it onto the decking as I stride up to her.

"You're lucky I'm weak right now, otherwise I would be burning your ass off this ship." I warn, bringing a silver flicker to Umber's eyes.

"No, I'm lucky because you value the fact I can provide information no one else has from *everywhere*, except for that fucking Mountain. You know you need me."

"I don't need you that bad." I say, raising my chin as I stare her down.
"Tell me to leave then." She retorts, and before I can do exactly that, a heap of sizzling bodies drop onto the main deck. Shouts and screams pierce my ears as I jump over the helm railing, landing onto the decking below. The crowd parts, save for the few Water Fae gathered by the near indiscernible bodies of my friends, the healers assessing the damage.

I drop to my knees, shakily reaching out a hand and halting abruptly. For the first time in my life, I have no idea what to do. A groan emits from Orion, his body trapped under Novak and Alvis' on top of him. I don't dare move anyone, their charred skin sloughing and angry flesh visible. I glance up to the four females kneeling in a semi circle around them, each of their brows furrowed.

Two have blue eyes and two have violet like the twins, though every pair is lit up as they stare past me into nothingness, their hands still shakily hovering over my family. Niamh, the only one who can speak, pulls out of her trance and focuses on me with seriousness masking her petite and usually happy features.

"We can heal the twins, but Novak is a different story. He has layers of injuries, those inflicted upon him with dark magic, and those inflicted by them." She gestures to the twins. "We can only fix the wounds dealt by fire and the twin's magic, the dark magic we cannot touch."

"Just do what you can, how much extra do you need?" I ask hastily, worried we won't have enough.

"It's hard to tell, have two flasks on hand in case. We will start here and move them to your cabin, yeah?" Niamh asks and I nod, grateful for her taking the lead.

"Umber-" I begin, but she is already directing the crew to makeshift together an infirmary in my quarters, clearing the area around us as well.

"Cap." Orion's hoarse voice jolts me and I lay down beside him. Novak's face is melded to Orion's dark chest, and Alvis' face is melted to Novak's back.

"Don't speak, you're safe." I murmur, wishing I could take his blistered hand. He shakes his head, wincing at the movement.

"No, we're not." Orion slurs, then passes out.

"Cap, you have to move." Umber says, a hand outstretched beside me. I take it and step back as everyone watches Niamh and the other healers work their magic. I squeeze Umber's hand and focus on her face, unable to watch burnt skin fall off and be replaced by fresh pink.

"Please don't leave." I whisper, and she nods, sapphire coils bouncing. "Do we have enough to get home?"

"I think so, if not home, at least out of Sylvan lands." Umber says.

"I will be incapacitated for the night, can you?" I ask, surprising alighting Umber's handsome face. She tugs on my hand and pulls me close, pressing her forehead to mine as the smell of flesh fills the incoming morning.

"Of course."

We stand like that for several minutes, unmoving until Niamh's tired voice perks my ears. "They can be moved."

I release Umber's hand and she leaves me for the helm, quietly ordering some of the less distracted crew members to assist her with take off. Several of the crew mates step forward to help the healer without being asked, pairs carefully situating themselves at heads and feet, lifting bodies onto makeshift stretchers. Novak's is the last and I follow behind.

"Novak will go on my bed, put the twins together there." I say, pointing to my bed and the mattress on the floor beside it, Alvis' from downstairs. Once everyone is settled, the crew mates wait just inside my door, fidgeting as they watch the healers resume their work.

"Will they be alright, Cap?" Russel asks, the kind and burly Earth Fae we picked up just a few months before Novak left. I sigh and rest a hand on his shoulder, the others close beside us.

"I don't know Rus, but I will do everything in my power to ensure they are. Crew is family, you know this." I say, locking eyes with each set of sullen and downcast eyes.

"If you need anything, please tell us." Vesper says, the youngest of our crew, an air Fae coming into their third decade. I rustle their shaggy silver hair and smile softly, which brings a glow to Vesper's near white eyes. That glow always brings me life, the Fae was a shell of their self when I found them.

"You know Ves, Umber is actually Captain tonight and is without a first mate, tell her I sent you, alright? If you're not tired, that is." I ramble on, bringing a smile to Vesper's thin lips revealing dimples similar to Novak's.

"Straightaway Captain!" Vesper announces, the first to leave my quarters. I thank the others and they leave, though Russel hovers for a moment longer.

"Really though, I'll be awake, so send if you need help." He offers.

"I do have a favor, but it will be when we land, so you might want your beauty rest." I say, and he raises a thick hazel brow.

"I need Lexeran, last I knew he was hanging out in the Mists. I need you to bring him to me."

"Didn't you have a falling out? What if he says no?" Russel asks, rubbing his broad chin. I groan and swipe raven hair away from my face.

"Tell him Novak needs him, and he'll be here." I decide and he nods, then presses a hand to his chest. "Thank you, Russel." Russel dips his head, then leaves, softly shutting the door behind him.

"Captain, we need more Aether." Niamh's exhausted voice spins me on my heel, her and the others are all working on Novak with pale faces and dull eyes. I spring for the safe under my desk, quickly unlocking it. I take four flasks, leaving only one left. I groan internally, it's taken so long for Orion and I to collect this much Aether thus far, and in a singular night all our reserves will be entirely gone.

I pass a flask to each of the females, though two of them are wary of the process. I gesture to Orion, skin no longer blistered but a new layer of angry pink, then to the flask in the healers hands.

"We found a way to 'donate' Aether, these quartz containers are the only thing that can reserve it, for times like this. Since it's not used by the body, you can theoretically store an unending amount of Aether without angering the Machine, but you can only intake what you are lacking, filling your magical pool to the brim and nothing more."

They nod in unison, then Niamh takes the lead and unscrews the cap from her flask. She inhales the glimmering lilac Aether as it drifts out with her eyes closed. The entire contents are emptied, like I figured they would be, and when Niamh's eyes are open they are renewed with a bright oceanic blue. She smiles at the others, which encourages them to follow suit. One by one I watch magic and life return to dulled eyes, and they bow their heads to me, then simultaneously sign 'thank you'.

I bring my flat palm to my lips, repeating the sign. "No, thank you." Warmth floods their cheeks, I have not learned the other's names and I'm not the type to pry, but Niamh has taught me some of the language over time in preparation for the day they wish to speak to me. I haven't asked Niamh why she kept her tongue and her companions did not, such questions are not my business.

As the Water Fae begin stitching together lacerations and bones on the twins and layering new skin on all three bodies, I find a bucket of water and a cloth. In silence I first wash Alvis once they are finished with him, then Orion as the healers combine their efforts to work on Novak. Their clothes are burnt and nearly non-existent. I debate sending someone below deck or going myself, but I find three sets of clothes neatly folded at the foot of my bed, must be Umber thought of everything.

By the time I'm done slipping loose tunics and trousers on the twins, carefully rolling them back and forth as I slide clothes on and providing them as much dignity as I can, the healers have finished with Novak, or at least I think.

"Why all the bandages?" I ask, leaving the twins bedside to survey over Niamh's hunched shoulders, aghast at Novak's state. She waves off her exhausted comrades who leave, but not before I show respect to each by pressing a fist to my hyper ventilating chest.

After the door shuts I take Novak's hand with great care, perhaps one of the few places that they could actually heal. His entire chest, shoulders and neck are bandaged, blood seeping through the linens. Bandages also wrap around his crown, bright red tainting the fabric covering his ears. His thready pulse echoes under my thumb caressing his wrist and I sigh, rubbing my face with my other hand.

"Do you know what the l'*aryik* ritual is?" Niamh asks softly and I shake my head, attention lingering on Novak's scrunched up brows. He's in pain, even in his sleep. "It's old magic, so evil and dark it was banished long ago, though of course such things don't matter to someone like Typhan. It appears that's what happened here." She gestures to Novak and I tilt my head.

"What does it mean?"

"It translates to The Banishing, a blood ritual only the most powerful Fae can carry out. It involves carving insignias into the body that drain the being of their Aether. They cannot be healed, or reversed by any means I am aware of, and it seems they ..." Niamh trails off and her eyes glisten as Novak stirs, then she starts again once he settles. "They rounded his ears, they didn't cut them off, just rounded them."

Red coats my vision and my heart races, threatening to implode with adrenaline. Typhan and his damn dogs, they've probably been waiting in the dark to strike when he's alone. I gently release Novak's hand and rest it along his side, then stand and take wavering steps around to the twins once more. I stare down at Alvis, other than their healing pink skin and bruising where flesh wasn't burnt, they look better.

"And these two?" I ask, attention on Alvis' hands as I notice black tainting his already dark fingertips. I kneel and carefully take his hand, which startles him awake. Hands desperately find my shoulders and wide violet eyes dart around the room.

"Safe. You're safe." I murmur, his jugular throbs wildly as his constricted pupils lock onto mine. "Orion is beside you, Novak is on the floor there, by dear Niamh." Novak's name snaps Alvis upwards in bed, resulting in dizziness clouding his eyes. I steady him before he falls over the edge, then wrap my arms around him and constrict tight.

"Breathe. Right now, everything is ok. Breathe, and tell me after."

Alvis' arms shakily wrap around my waist and I rest my chin on his head, still tightly embracing him. Sobs wrack his body and I close my eyes, inhaling through my nose to calm rising anger at Typhan and whatever new monster he's employed to hurt my family. Niamh sits cross legged in her wooden chair, eyes closed as she waits patiently by Novak's side. Tear by tear, Alvis regains himself. After long minutes of air catching in his slowly calming lungs, he pulls from my chest and looks up to me with swollen eyes.

"Alvis, who did this to you?" I ask, brows furrowed as I wipe tears from both his eyes with careful thumbs. The white bonds along his neck glow a blinding white as emotions overtake him once more. He takes my hand and stares directly in my eyes, hot sadness dripping off his quivering lips.

"He killed everyone, the entire village, all of the *Nafshyi*, he nearly had O and I." Alvis chokes on his last words and I cup his cheek, impatience creeping under my skin. Before I can ask once more, he gains courage. "Novak, he killed everyone."

My ears ring as nausea sweeps up my throat, the embers coming to life in my eyes reflect in the glistening of Alvis' dulled violet. "What are you talking about?"

"It's true." Orion sputters hoarsely, clasping his side with a shaky hand, eyes closed.

"O! I'm so glad you're okay, what happened after I-"

"Stop." I order, body crawling with anxiety and confusion, ants toiling under my skin and burrowing into my muscles. This cannot be true, the young hero I've spent my life protecting, caring for. This cannot be. "Start over."

Orion sits up on a elbow with great difficulty and faces me, resting on the opposite side of Alvis. Niamh clears her throat and stands. "There is nothing more I can do tonight. May I be excused?"

"Yes, I am sorry for keeping you, I will compensate you for your services in the morning." I say hurriedly and her brows furrow, full lips open but I raise a hand. "I pay you to heal idiots from drunken brawls, not this kind of disaster. You and your friends will be compensated for keeping my family alive, end of discussion."

Niamh smiles softly and bows her head to me, then repeats the motion to each of the confused twins before taking her leave. "Niamh said those *Nafshyi* roughed our mate up here pretty bad before you got there, some ritual called the Banishing?"

The twins simultaneously blanch and tighten their fists. "No. No. No." Alvis repeats defiantly, raking a trembling hand through his coils.

"His ears are cut too, aren't they?" Orion asks, which snaps his brother's attention to him. I nod, throat burning my grief. "Then it's personal, I bet those *Nafshyi* had ties to Loyska."

"Well, he's not empty, that's for sure." Alvis mutters and my ears perk. "We didn't even know it *was* Novak until the end, there's something *using* him."

"Using him?" I lean back on my heels.

"Like a shadow Ancient, or demon, *something* I've never seen before, *what* it is I don't know. What I do know is it's incredibly powerful and pissed off, and it doesn't like us. If we weren't so drained, it probably wouldn't have been so difficult."

"The more damage we inflicted the more control it lost and by the end, it was Novak's body, but with the eyes of the demon. It said it had fun *playing* and we could have him back for now, which leads me to believe we have a ticking time bomb on this ship."

I rub my chin, contemplating Orion's words. Alvis stares at his clenched hands and I pretend not to notice the blood trickling from his palms. "What are you suggesting, brother?" He snaps.

"Don't get pissy with me, you didn't almost kill our first mate. That is not an experience I want to repeat again." Orion retorts, hackles rising and eyes flickering with dim lilac. Alvis sulks, crossing his arms. I stand and raise my palms.

"You three dropped onto this ship in a ball of flames, nearly dead. Quit your bickering and get some rest. I believe for now, we can do that."

The twins glance at each other with softened faces and clasp hands, then nod. "Fine, but have your bed back." Alvis say, flinching as he thinks about moving. I wave him off, then trace over to Novak's side. I pull the chairs together so I can sit in one with my feet up on the other.

"This is where I want to be." I whisper and glance down at Novak's pained features after I settle, but Alvis' stare catches my attention.

"Do you really think he's going to be ok?" Alvis whispers, sitting up on an elbow. I stare back down at Novak, contemplating what to say that will resonate some shred of truth. If Novak remembers everything when he wakes up, I don't put it past him to try and disappear again.

"*Hakol missetader kemo shetsarikhe,*" I murmur. Memories of my mother brushing my smooth hair as we watch the sandy world outside our front door swims in my broken heart. "Everything has a way of working out."

What I need.

Alvis

"Look at what you've done to him. Another victim to your treacherous bloodline."

The Shadow is in all it's full glory, blood drips from it's rows of teeth cutting through strangling pitch black darkness. Shimmering talons extend from his humanoid arm and twist in Novak's hair, dangling his body off the ground. White vines thrust from the ground and imprison me, forcing me to my knees as Novak stares into my eyes.

"Why didn't you ask me to stay?" He asks, blood gurgling from his lips as the claws penetrate through his vocal chords. I scream but it's soundless, the only noise that meets my ears is the snapping of Novak's neck, then the thud of his body hitting the ground as rows of demonic teeth devour my face.

I jolt out of the nightmare in a cold sweat, heart shivering and wild eyes immediately focusing on the door left open a crack. Orion and Captain are soundlessly sleeping, but Novak is gone. I crawl out of bed and nearly fall forwards when my feet touch the floor, the ship is thrashing against steady rain. No one is screaming and we're in flight, so Novak can't have gotten very far, and must be himself. I'm already

173

dressed in a loose casual outfit of linens, mustiness meets my senses as I pull the navy blue fabric of the long sleeve to my face. I look around the room quickly but don't find a jacket in immediate sight.

I shut the door softly behind me, a wintry mix of ice and rain pelleting my face the moment I step onto the main decking. I stand by the mainmast and scan my surroundings, eyes catching on a soaking wet Umber steering the ship through wet evening. She silently raises a sapphire finger to the crows nest above and I press my fist to my chest in acknowledgment before climbing the slick foremast rigging.

The higher I climb more fear crawls up my neck and rattles my ears, but I don't like the fact he's up here alone in this state, and this weather. I climb into modest size bucket of a crow's nest, finding Novak circling the tapered mast with rapidly flashing colors riding through his eyes, alternating between all shades of blue and black.

"Hey." I murmur and he stumbles backwards. I shakily stand feet away from him, the put my hands up.

"Don't come any closer!" Novak cries, voice broken and words lost with the thunder cracking in the distance.

"You're safe, Nova, hear me? Take a breath, talk to me." I drop my hands, heart cracking to see him in this state. The multitude of bandages encircling his torso, arms and neck have soaked through with blood. Sleet filled rain allows crimson to flow freely down his body, mixing with his matted hair and the fabric of his trousers.

"*Nonononononono.*" He repeats manically, hands twisting in his hair. I swallow a hard lump of fear, insanity overwhelms his skeletal features, was he this malnourished before?

I extend my hand tom him and he jolts backwards as if I've struck him, knuckles blanch as he clutches to the railing he nearly topples over. "Alvis, please just stop!" Novak shudders, tears stream down his red face with black eyes cast downwards. "I don't want to hurt you."

"Nova, I won't ever stop trying to help you." I admit through angry tears, inky coils catching wind. I recompose myself, shaky hands raking the length of my hair back. I haven't cut my hair or trimmed my face since he's left. "I'm sorry, Novak, but I won't stop caring for you. I don't care what's happened between us, did you not get my letter?" Novak's hands drop into fists and his mood shifts as he surprisingly closes the distance between us. "What was I supposed to do, come back crawling hoping you'd forgive me? You don't deserve that shit!" His cracking shout cuts over the building wind and my eyes burn bright, a violet glow lighting the storm around us. Lightning sparks over the nearing mainland, we really shouldn't be up here. I step closer and rest my hands on his shoulders, which relax at once.

"You wouldn't have had to crawl. I meant what I said, I'm always here for you, whatever you need me to be." I whisper, brushing knotted locks of filthy blonde away from his eyes. Novak looks up to me with eyes the color of night. His cheeks warm against the icy rain as I release hope into the wind. "Is that what you were hoping for, to be in my arms again?"

Novak stares into my soul in silence, searching for something. Selfish hope glimmers in my shameless spirit. I don't care if he hurts me again, I don't care what I have to do or what I have to face. I love him.

"I don't want to be with anyone, for the rest of my life." Novak states defiantly, stepping out of my grasp. My hands rest into fists at my side and I reel in my pain fueled Aether, magic already building in the few hours rest I've had.

"That's a bit of a ridiculous statement, if you don't love me anymore then just say it Nova. I can handle it." I pinch the bridge of my nose, cursing myself for slipping with the old name that makes him flinch.

"I don't want to be with *anyone* Alvis. If she'll have me, I'm going to stay on the ship, where Captain can keep an eye on me. If you really mean it, you'll stay here, as my friend, because that's what I need. This thing, I can't let it escape again." Novak turns away and crosses his arms, inhaling frozen wetness so deeply his entire bloodied torso rises with the breath.

I stare down at my saturated leather boots, playing over every moment we've had together since we've met. Given what's happened, it's selfish of me to expect he can have room for this. We've saved each other so many times, loved each other in so many different ways. Can I really go back to playing the role of friend without spiraling into a dark hell of my own?

I raise my eyes to Novak, trembling in the storm. I step forward and gently sling an arm around his shoulder, then look down to his surprised face. He expected me to leave, and the relief that washes over his eyes that brighten from black to blue in my presence is enough to make me follow him anywhere, no matter what.

"Whatever you need me to be, I'm here."

About the Author

What happens when you mix a debut fantasy author with waves of young witch vibes, endless coffee stains and a love for adventure? Living in the Adirondacks of Northern New York, Aelina's work is heavily influenced by her love for the outdoors and high stakes adventures filled with angst and love. The Eternal Machine is the first novel in the trilogy, Take Me to Iverbourne.

You can connect with me on:

🌐 https://linktr.ee/aelinaisaacs

Also by Aelina Isaacs

Take me to Iverbourne is a dark steampunk fantasy series which includes novellas focusing on different character's backstories and provides vital clues for the next adventure in the Realm of Giants.

Children of Iverbourne

Children of Iverbourne is a prequel novella taking place 236 years before The Eternal Machine, following the original heroes of the war torn lands and the difficult choices they must make, all to ensure a better future.

A terrified **slave**, lacking bravery or free will, sent on an impossible journey.

A hardened **Commander** of the Eternal prison, taking in his newest inmate. An hours old baby.

A half crazed Fae, **former Hero** of Borealis, Court of the Humans.

Two Parents on a journey to deliver their child to Iverbourne, to **freedom**, no matter the cost.

A new Captain, and a trouble making Water Fae with a constant smirk.

Prince of Sylvan

Prince of Sylvan is a prequel novella taking place twenty years before The Eternal Machine.

Alvis is the preferred heir to the throne of Sylvan, a **Fae** court built on hatred and blood. High Lord Typhan pushes Alvis every day to **murder** his own brother and absorb his power, becoming an unstoppable **weapon**.

A lifelong **blood** bond will force Alvis to make a choice between his brother or mother, as he cannot **disobey** a command given by his father. Unlike most blood bonds, his can be broken, at the **expense** of his mother's life.

Typhan is losing patience and soon his request will be a **command**, then Alvis will have to kill his kin by the **sword**, or a broken blood bond. Alvis decides he would rather take his **own life** than choose between his kin and live as a **monster** any longer, but a legendary **Captain** arrives with a troublesome first mate the Prince can't keep out of his **heart**.

Friends, love and a whole new world waits outside their imprisoned court, but at what cost?

Blood, or **sanity**?

The Eternal Machine

Keeper of Death is quite a fitting name for a villain, and yet Lythienne finds herself as the only Fae who can save the realm of Iverbourne.

Born as an Empty Fae, she is sent into the Eternal Mountain, a prison designed for the most malicious, blood thirsty and cursed creatures alive. Her crime, along with so many other creatures, is being Lesser than the grand High Fae who rule the divided lands above.

Aether magic rules Iverbourne, a whimsical land ravaged by long held prejudices, unkind to all those without magic. The Others are a mysterious court to the south, kidnapping and murdering all those on their path through the continent.

Only a Fae without Aether can wield the mysterious Harbinger, a weapon of mass destruction needed to defeat the epic evil taking over the realm. The elegant call of immense power corrupts most, especially those who have been mistreated.

Dangerous lust, high stakes adventure and loyal companionship are thrust into Lyth's life, but can she be the Hero after playing the Villain for so long? After all, why would you want to save a world that wants to see you buried six feet under?

Perhaps this isn't a hero saves the day story. Perhaps, this is the origin story of the Deadliest Fae alive.

Realm of Giants

Realm of Giants releases in February of 2022.

Novak. Zemer. Akar. Tzel. Vagabond Bard.

I've had many names throughout my life, and I suppose they've all suited me well enough. Who knew Villain would be the name that I wear best?

Months after the events in The Eternal Machine, Novak leads an Expedition into the long separated Realm of Giants, a land filled with dragons and dangerous secret societies who already have their eyes set on Iverbourne.

Novak's mind is set on one thing, defying the course of Death, but as he meets new foes, finds family and himself, he begins to ask himself a vital question.

Is defying Death worth the cost of humanity?

Made in the USA
Monee, IL
06 May 2022

96013607R00114